"You have, I understand, been hired to guard my body for twenty-four hours a day?"

"Yes, technically speaking, I suppose I have. But…"

"Well, there you are!" Lorenzo grinned wolfishly down at her. "I suddenly realized that it would be churlish, to say the least, to turn down the opportunity of having *you*, my dear Antonia, closely guarding my body through the night."

"You must be joking!" she laughed.

But, as Antonia discovered for the second time that evening, she was guilty of seriously underestimating an opponent, as Lorenzo suddenly moved at what seemed to be the speed of light. A nanosecond later, she found herself firmly clasped by one steely, unyielding arm while he placed his other hand firmly under her chin.

As he tilted her face up toward him, she barely had time to become aware of his blue eyes glittering down at her, before his dark head was descending swiftly toward her, his mouth possessing her lips in a kiss of devastating intensity.

MARY LYONS was born in Toronto, Canada, moving to live permanently in England when she was six, although she still proudly maintains her Canadian citizenship. Having married and raised four children, her life nowadays is relatively peaceful—unlike her early years when she worked as a radio announcer, reviewed books and, for a time, lived in a turbulent area of the Middle East. She still enjoys a bit of excitement, combining romance with action, humor and suspense in her books whenever possible.

Books by Mary Lyons

Don't miss any of our special offers. Write to us at the following address for information on our newest releases.

Harlequin Reader Service
U.S.: 3010 Walden Ave., P.O. Box 1325, Buffalo, NY 14269
Canadian: P.O. Box 609, Fort Erie, Ont. L2A 5X3

Mary Lyons

THE ITALIAN SEDUCTION

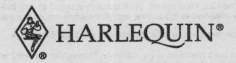

HARLEQUIN®

TORONTO • NEW YORK • LONDON
AMSTERDAM • PARIS • SYDNEY • HAMBURG
STOCKHOLM • ATHENS • TOKYO • MILAN • MADRID
PRAGUE • WARSAW • BUDAPEST • AUCKLAND

ISBN 0-373-12120-2

THE ITALIAN SEDUCTION

First North American Publication 2000.

Copyright © 2000 by Mary Lyons.

Visit us at www.eHarlequin.com

Printed in U.S.A.

CHAPTER ONE

'LORENZO—you really *must* be sensible! You could be in grave danger.'

'Nonsense!'

Standing behind his large desk, Lorenzo Foscari gave a brief, slightly irritated shrug of his broad shoulders as he continued to toss files and papers into an open briefcase. 'Quite frankly, Matteo, I consider that you, and the other directors of this company, are taking these foolish threats far too seriously.'

Matteo Barocci gave a heavy sigh, before once again trying to persuade the younger man to see sense.

Unfortunately, it clearly wasn't going to be an easy task. Which was hardly surprising. After all, no man of thirty-eight—let alone a good-looking, wealthy bachelor with a host of glamorous girlfriends—was likely to welcome having his private life seriously curtailed.

However, as a director of a large industrial corporation—of which Lorenzo was chairman and managing director—Matteo could only agree with the firm's insurance company when they'd insisted that action must be taken immediately.

'In the event of anything happening to Signor Foscari, we would be called upon to pay out a huge sum of money to your company. Which is why we cannot afford to take any risks, and are insisting that he has close protection, at all times, until there is no longer any threat to his life.'

But it was one thing for the insurance company to lay down the law, Matteo told himself with another, heavy sigh and quite another to persuade Lorenzo to accept measures designed to protect him. All the same...he had no choice but to try.

'Now, Lorenzo—you must listen to reason,' he pleaded. 'Because, however "foolish" it may seem to you, once someone has written letters threatening your life, it would be the height of folly to take no notice of such a warning.'

'*Sì, d'accordo*...I agree. You are quite right to insist that I take sensible precautions,' Lorenzo said, placing his passport in the case, before firmly closing the lid. 'And that's precisely what I intend to do.'

'So, you'll agree to have a bodyguard, and...'

'Absolutely not.' Lorenzo shook his dark head as he pressed down the intercom, asking his secretary to notify the chauffeur that he was about to leave the building. 'While I am quite prepared to be careful, I refuse to believe that I am in any immediate danger. Certainly *not* enough to warrant the appointment of a bodyguard!'

'But our insurers and the other directors of the company are insisting that...'

'Damn it, Matteo!' Lorenzo grated, his blue eyes glinting with anger and frustration. 'We both know that the man was nothing but a thief. A loathsome little man who, in his role of chief accountant, betrayed our trust by stealing tens of millions of lire from this company, before I sacked him. Right?'

'Quite right. But...'

'Yes...yes, I know that he's apparently made threats against my life,' Lorenzo added impatiently. 'But I fail to understand why everyone seems to be taking him seriously.'

'I've already explained that...'

'Oh, come on! Giovanni may have been a crooked, greedy man, who had no scruples about robbing this company. But the idea that he's suddenly become a dangerous assassin is totally absurd!'

Continuing to ignore the older man's protests, he picked up his briefcase from the desk, moving swiftly across the thick carpet towards the door of his large, spacious office.

'For instance, I very much doubt if Giovanni would even recognise a gun when he saw one—let alone know how to fire it. Which is why the idea that I now need a body-guard—to protect me from such a puny, insignificant little man—is utter nonsense!'

'But…but the insurance company is insisting that you…you *must* take precautions,' Matteo protested breath-lessly, almost having to run to keep up with the other man's tall, slim figure as Lorenzo left his office, and began strid-ing quickly down the marble-floored corridor, towards his personal elevator.

'For how long would I be expected to put up with this bodyguard? One month? Six months? A year?'

'Well…er…I really don't know,' Matteo muttered help-lessly. 'It could be for some time, I suppose.'

'That is precisely the conclusion I'd come to,' Lorenzo snapped as the elevator doors opened and he entered the steel cage, closely followed by his colleague. So as far as I'm concerned you can forget it! Because I'm damned if I'll put up with being forced to live—for who knows what length of time?—with some empty-brained, muscle-bound gorilla!'

It was now far too late, of course, Lorenzo told himself grimly, his lips tightening with exasperation as the lift hur-tled down, towards the ground floor of the large office building. It was *far* too late to regret not calling in the police when he'd first been informed by the auditors of a serious problem in the company's financial department. Prompt and swift action, at that point, would undoubtedly have saved everyone a considerable amount of time and trouble.

Unfortunately, instead of being sensible, he'd allowed his compassion to overcome his better judgement.

After calling the chief accountant, Giovanni Parini, into his office and tearing him off a strip, Lorenzo had been disconcerted and embarrassed when the man had broken down—not only admitting his guilt, but weeping with distress about the future welfare of his wife and many small children. Which was why, very stupidly, Lorenzo had merely called Security to have the man immediately escorted from the building.

What an idiot he'd been! Because it had soon become evident that there was no wife and definitely no small children. In fact, Giovanni, who'd been living alone with his comfortably off, elderly mother, had now disappeared and was on the run. But not before leaving behind him a letter, threatening to kill Lorenzo—the one person who'd been foolish enough to show him some clemency.

Which only serves you right, for being such a soft touch! Lorenzo told himself grimly. However…if he now had the opportunity to get his hands around the thin, scrawny neck of the company's late and entirely unlamented chief accountant, he'd have *great* pleasure in cheerfully squeezing the life from the wretched man!

'You really cannot continue ignoring the demands of our insurance company.'

'Hmm…?'

Preoccupied in cursing himself for having been so lenient, Lorenzo realised that he'd missed part of what his companion had been saying.

'What demands?' he queried as the elevator doors opened, and he began walking across the foyer, towards the main doors of the large office block.

'You clearly haven't been listening to what I've been saying!' his colleague protested, hurrying after the taller man as Lorenzo swept through the glass doors to where his uniformed chauffeur was standing beside a large black limousine.

'Our insurers are adamant that you must have the protection of a bodyguard, at all times, until Giovanni Parini is caught,' Matteo continued breathlessly.

'What nonsense!' Lorenzo grated as he came to an abrupt

halt, spinning around on his heels to glare down at the other man. 'Are you seriously trying to tell me...?'

Matteo nodded quickly. 'They say if you don't take their advice—especially as you will be travelling abroad for the next couple of weeks or so—they will immediately withdraw your insurance cover.'

'This is totally ridiculous!' Lorenzo exclaimed angrily. 'How can they *seriously* believe that Giovanni is likely to be dogging my footsteps around Europe? My schedule has not yet been finalised. So where and how would he get the information about my business meetings in Switzerland, Germany and Britain? How could he know where I will be on any one, particular day—when I don't yet have that information myself?'

Matteo shrugged. 'It seems they regard you as being vitally important for the future of this company. Which is why they are not prepared to take any risks whatsoever—and will cancel the policy unless you agree to their terms.'

Swearing violently under his breath, Lorenzo stared grimly down at the other man for a moment, before quickly glancing at the slim gold watch on his wrist.

'If I don't hurry, I'm going miss my flight to Zurich. Which means that I've no time to hang around arguing about this subject any longer,' he grated angrily, handing his briefcase to the chauffeur before climbing into the passenger seat at the rear of the vehicle.

'I'm sorry...' Matteo sighed. 'Believe me, I have tried to reason with the insurers. But, while they aren't prepared to take even the slightest risk of anything happening to you, they have agreed to make the arrangements regarding your bodyguard. Apparently they expect to have someone in place by the time you reach London. And they have also agreed to pay all the fees involved.'

'I should damn well hope so!' Lorenzo retorted through clenched teeth. 'Especially when I think of the huge sums we've paid our insurers over the years. Nothing short of daylight robbery!' he exploded, before taking a deep breath and making an effort to calm down.

'I want you to make something very clear to our insurance company,' he continued grimly, slamming the car door shut with a bang, before lowering his window to deliver a parting shot. '*If* they're twisting my arm, and forcing me to have a bodyguard, they'd better make certain that he's the very best in the business!'

Over six hundred miles and many light-years away from the sophisticated city of Milan, Antonia Simpson gave a heavy sigh as she leaned back in the front passenger seat of the chauffeur-driven Rolls-Royce.

Gazing longingly out of the window at the bright sunshine, and the light breeze rustling the leaves of the trees at the edge of the airfield, she found herself thinking that it was about time she had a break.

It was all very well running one's own business. And she certainly was making a considerable amount of money. But the unrelenting pressure of always having to be totally alert and aware of danger, at all times, was beginning to wear her down.

Which was ridiculous, really, because she'd spent the last eleven years thoroughly enjoying all aspects of her job—eleven years into which she'd packed more adventures than most people experienced in a lifetime.

She'd always been a tomboy, of course. Which wasn't exactly surprising, since following her mother's death, when Antonia was only a few months old, her father had raised her in exactly the same way as he'd done her three older brothers. And he'd been delighted to discover, as the years went by, that she was the only one of his children to inherit his natural aptitude for sports.

There was a downside to her happy, comfortable childhood, of course. For instance, it had been a shock, at the age of sixteen, to discover that men preferred girls who wore frilly frocks. And as she'd grown older she'd been confused to discover that most of her brothers' male friends—however nice they might be—didn't take kindly to being beaten hollow at tennis. Nor did they like being told not to be 'sloppy'—and quickly tossed, judo-style, over her shoulder whenever they tried to kiss her.

However, on leaving school and training as a fitness instructor, it was when she was asked to help look after one of her students—who'd suddenly achieved unexpected fame as a rock star—that she'd discovered her true vocation, taking up 'close protection' as a permanent job. By which time, of course, she'd also discovered that being kissed by the opposite sex wasn't really quite so bad, after all! Which hadn't been much of a help when she was chosen to join a training course with the SAS.

Antonia still shuddered at the memory of those harsh, desperately exhausting few weeks, which she'd spent at a secret location in Herefordshire. The only woman on the course, she was never quite sure how she'd managed to survive the brutally tough regime—a postgraduate course in advanced security techniques, which had dramatically changed her life—and resulted in her becoming a highly valued member of her chosen profession.

But…well, there had been many times, lately, when she had found herself wondering what it would be like to live an ordinary, normal, everyday life.

Which was one of the reasons that she'd recently formed her own, private security firm. Specialising in various training courses—both for members of the general public, as well as employees of various security firms—she also provided clients with surveillance teams for an assortment of mundane problems, such as internal theft and the prevention of industrial espionage.

It was certainly a lot quieter and more peaceful than some of the jobs she'd had in the past. But Antonia was beginning to think that maybe, somewhere along the line, she'd somehow managed to miss out on something vital.

Most of her friends were married, and had happily settled down to enjoy family life. And, although she was definitely not looking for a husband—and hadn't even begun to think about having any children of her own—she was becoming increasingly aware of strange feelings of dissatisfaction with her life, which she had absolutely no idea how to combat.

Possibly the answer to her problems was simply that she needed a holiday. While she was not someone who enjoyed lying around on a sandy beach for any length of time, the idea of renting a villa, high in the hills of Greece or Italy, was definitely appealing.

Antonia was just anticipating the future delights of enjoying fresh mountain air, and of strolling through fragrant pine woods, when her thoughts were interrupted as the Rolls-Royce came slowly, and sedately, to a halt.

'Get a grip, Harold! You really must try to do better than this! How many times do I have to tell you: at the first sign of a deliberate obstruction you *immediately* slam the gear into reverse—and stamp down *hard* on the accelerator?'

'Yes, I know, miss,' the chauffeur muttered unhappily. 'But I can't seem to bring myself to harm the car, somehow.'

'OK...' Antonia sighed. 'I know it's hard to break the habits of a lifetime. But if it's a case of worrying about your vehicle, or saving the life of your passenger—there's really no choice, is there? So, let's try it again, shall we?'

Harold sighed heavily. He was clearly hating every minute of the course, designed to teach chauffeurs of rich and influential businessmen how to escape from tricky situations.

'That was *much* better! You're really getting the hang of it,' Antonia told him encouragingly some minutes later as the large vehicle juddered abruptly to a halt at the sight of a car, suddenly blocking its path, before racing backwards down the tarmac at a rate of knots.

'Now, I'm going to let you continue on your own,' she added, unbuckling her seat belt. 'I want you to keep going around the circuit until you can instinctively react to a problem, without having to stop and think what to do. And then one of my assistants will give you some practice in controlling a skid on roads which have been deliberately sprayed with oil. OK?'

He nodded, looking far more cheerful than he had earlier as she got out of the car, and began walking over the long grass towards a large, decrepit building on the far side of the old East Anglign airfield—an ancient relic of World War II.

When the sun was shining, England in June was just about perfect, Antonia told herself, taking off her crash helmet and shaking free her shoulder-length blonde hair. However, just as she was relishing both the smell of new-mown hay from a nearby field and the chirping of birds, wheeling and diving in the sky, far above her head, she was recalled to more mundane matters by the imperative buzz of her mobile phone.

Recognising the number on the back-lit display as that of James Riley, an old colleague who was now running a top security agency, Antonia took a deep breath before answering his call. James could be very persuasive, but there was *no way* she was going to allow him to cajole or sweet-talk her into taking on another of his rotten jobs.

'I'm definitely *not* interested in guarding any more Arab princesses,' she announced grimly, before he had a chance to say anything. 'Your last client was a totally manic sho-paholic! In fact, if I *never* have to visit Knightsbridge or Bond Street again, as long as I live, that's just fine by me!'

'Hang about, Tony!' he protested. 'It's nothing like that.'

'Oh, yeah? Well, just as long as you've got the message,' she told him firmly. 'Besides, I'm running my own business these days. And I've got more work than I know what to do with. So...'

'Hey—relax. You're quite right,' he murmured soothingly. 'I'll admit that I shouldn't have lumbered you with that job. It was just a mistake, OK? Definitely not right for someone of your experience and expertise. After all, you're one of the best in the business. Right?'

'*Uh-oh*...this is beginning to sound like some of your usual, lousy soft-soap, James!' she retorted warily. 'When you start paying compliments, I just *know* that you've got a dirty job lined up for me. So, what is it this time? Going undercover to track down industrial espionage in a smelly chemical factory? Or tailing a suspect in a particularly nasty and brutal drug syndicate? Come on—spill the beans!'

'You've got it all wrong,' he told her in an aggrieved tone of voice. 'In fact, what I'm offering you is a really cushy, very simple job. Merely looking after a high-profile client, in a London hotel, for about ten days. Absolutely nothing to it. As easy as falling off a log,' he added quickly. 'And the fee you'll be getting is pretty spectacular, as well.'

'So—what's the catch?' she demanded.

'There isn't one,' he assured her earnestly. 'Believe me—it's a doddle.'

'Hmm!' she murmured suspiciously. 'The thing is, James, I can't help wondering—if it's really going to be as easy as you say—why you've bothered to contact me?'

'Well...the truth is...' He gave a heavy sigh. 'You're right. I did have Pete Davis lined up for the job. But the stupid man fell asleep at the wheel when driving home last night. And now he's in hospital with all his limbs in plaster.'

'So...?'

'So I can't get hold of anyone else who'd be suitable for the job, at such short notice,' James admitted bluntly. 'The client isn't the man you'd be guarding. It's his insurance company. *He* isn't taking the threats against his life seriously, but *they* are. Right? So, if the guy is to have close protection—apparently he's Italian, and not at all keen on the idea of a bodyguard—it has to be someone who's able to merge into his very up-market, social scene, and not stand out like a sore thumb. Which is where you come in. Because, from our enquiries so far, it seems that he's a bit of a womaniser.'

'Gee—thanks!'

'Nothing you can't handle,' James told her quickly. 'Just partial to the ladies...lots of glamorous girlfriends...you know the sort of thing.'

'Yes, unfortunately, I do,' she retorted grimly. 'OK, let's get down to brass tacks. What's the fee for the job?'

When James mentioned a sum she gave a hoot of grim laughter. 'Forget it!'

'Oh, come on, Tony. Don't give me a bad time.'

'What "bad time"? *I'm* the one who's going to have the hassle of dealing with a guy who, according to you, is "partial to the ladies". Which, if my past experience is anything to go by, means nothing but trouble. So, if you want me, you'll have to double that figure, make all the initial arrangements, *and* provide a specialist team for round-the-clock-surveillance—or I'm simply not interested.'

'You're a hard woman!' he groaned, before eventually and most reluctantly agreeing to her terms.

Lorenzo gave a sigh of relief as he gazed around his spacious hotel suite. After so many intensive, if stimulating business meetings in Zurich and Bonn, he was now looking forward to spending a more relaxing time in London.

Feeling hot and sticky, he slipped off the jacket of his dark suit, loosening his tie and stretching his long rangy body as he decided that, before having a shower, what he *really* needed was a stiff drink.

Even when travelling first-class, air travel these days was becoming increasingly tedious. It was ridiculous to be forced to spend so many long, boring hours in various terminals—especially when the flights themselves took hardly any time at all. With his company's business expanding so fast nowadays, maybe it was about time he acquired a private jet?

Luckily, he had only one meeting scheduled here in London, with a large private merchant bank, mainly concerning the funding of a new factory in the north of England. Which meant that he would have plenty of time to see his friends, and also visit his young niece, currently attending a language school in Cambridge.

But first of all, he reminded himself grimly, he was going to have to sort out this stupid business of being forced to put up with a bodyguard.

In regular touch with his office in Milan, he'd been informed by his secretary that the insurance company seemed to have pulled out all the stops. Not only had they appointed someone from a top security agency to look after him here in England, but they'd apparently sent his office a fax, demanding exhaustive details of his personal life.

Admittedly, some of the requests—a photocopy of his passport; his blood group; his height and weight and the name and address of his doctor in Milan—could possibly be regarded as sensible. Especially if he was likely to be in any danger—which, of course, he wasn't.

However, he deeply resented some of the other questions, such as: 'Does he have any aliases?' and 'Is he on a known hit list? Or affiliated with any political group?'

Who on earth did they think he was…James Bond?

In fact, Lorenzo told himself, slowly sipping his whisky and staring moodily out of the large, floor-to-ceiling windows at the traffic swirling around Hyde Park Corner, the whole business was obviously becoming a total farce.

And if this bodyguard…what was his name? He turned to pick up the message from Worldwide Security Inc., which he'd been handed on his arrival at the hotel. If this man, Tony Simpson, thought that Lorenzo was prepared to meekly accept being closely shadowed day and night, he was very much mistaken!

He'd had time, over the past few days, to give the matter some thought, and it looked as if his best solution to the problem would be to simply outbid the insurance company, by offering to double or even treble Mr Simpson's salary—provided he would leave Lorenzo alone. A decision, he told himself, which had the great virtue of both simplicity—and a way in which to satisfy the needs of everyone concerned.

Some time later, after deciding to forgo a shower in favour of a long, leisurely bath, Lorenzo found himself feeling a good deal more cheerful.

He'd obviously been in danger of allowing himself to become far too obsessed about having to put up with a bodyguard, he told himself ruefully as his long, tanned fingers quickly knotted his black bow-tie.

In fact, he'd do better to concentrate on the pleasure of renewing his acquaintance, this evening, with some old friends—who'd been kind enough to invite him to join them at the Albert Hall for a gala performance of excerpts from Verdi's opera *Otello*.

While he was smiling at the idea of an Italian travelling hundreds of miles to attend a performance of one of his own country's famous composers, Lorenzo's thoughts were sharply interrupted by the sound of a loud knock on the door of his suite.

Walking over to open the door, and fully expecting to see a member of the hotel staff—or the chauffeur of the limousine which had been placed at his disposal during his visit to London—Lorenzo was surprised to find himself staring down into the cool grey eyes of a tall, slim young woman.

'Signor Foscari?'

'*Sì*,' he responded, before quickly realising that the female standing in front of him was clearly English. 'Yes…yes, I am Lorenzo Foscari. Can I be of any assistance?' he added politely.

'Well…I think that it's probably the other way round,' she said with a quick smile, before putting out her hand towards him. 'I'm Antonia Simpson. I believe you are expecting me.'

Momentarily confused by the fact that she obviously knew his name, Lorenzo found himself automatically shaking the proffered hand, his puzzlement increasing as she gave him another brief smile, before moving swiftly past his tall figure and entering the large sitting room.

'This is all very comfortable,' she commented, quickly scanning the room with its deep sofas and large armchairs, whose pale cream upholstery matched the off-white raw silk curtains surrounding the tall windows. 'And you've got a great view of both Aspley House and Hyde Park Corner, haven't you?' she added, moving over to gaze out of the tall windows.

'Yes, it seems I have,' he murmured, leaning casually against the architrave of the open doorway of the sitting room, and regarding his unknown visitor with some amusement.

Lorenzo had travelled widely around the world on business over the past few years. Which was why his first, instinctive reaction to the sudden appearance of a strange female at the door of his suite had been to immediately assume that she was up to no good. Mainly, of course, because loose women frequently plied their trade in the world's top hotels—despite all attempts by respectable hoteliers to keep them well away from their premises.

However, after a long, searching glance at the slim, well-dressed figure in front of him, he swiftly discarded that notion.

With a mother and two much older sisters—not to mention a considerable number of sophisticated girlfriends—he knew enough about women's apparel to immediately recognise the hallmark design of a very expensive handbag, hanging from her shoulder on its thin gold chain. Moreover, the scoop-necked, sleeveless black silk cocktail dress—expertly cut to skim lightly over the curves of her tall, athletic body—clearly hadn't come cheap, either.

In fact, from the tips of her toes in those high-heeled shoes, up to the discreet sparkle of small diamond earrings, half hidden behind her shoulder-length blonde hair, this young woman was clearly a class act. So...what on earth was she doing here?

Standing across the room and taking a good, hard look at her new client, Antonia found herself feeling both surprised and slightly taken aback. Not merely because this man seemed to have an almost perfect command of the English language, with only a slight accent betraying his country of origin. Or the fact that he was so tall—most Italians of her acquaintance being far shorter and more rotund.

It was just...well...there hadn't been time for the agency to send her a photograph, of course. However, while she wouldn't have described him as classically handsome—not with that long aquiline nose and those high cheekbones—there was no doubt that Signor Foscari was a quite *amazingly* attractive man.

Maybe it was something to do with the hint of laughter glinting from beneath his heavy eyelids, thickly fringed with long black lashes? Or the warm, amused curve of his lips? But, even on the other side of this large room, she was almost physically aware of the highly potent, heady attraction of rampant sex appeal, which seemed to ooze from every pore of his tall, slim figure.

Trust that idiot James Riley to have got hold of the wrong end of the stick! Because she hadn't a moment's doubt that if this Italian was 'partial to the ladies' it was because they'd undoubtedly been throwing themselves at him ever since he'd put on his first pair of long trousers!

All the same…while few things fazed her nowadays, she definitely didn't like the way this man was looking at her. Maybe James hadn't been entirely off-beam, Antonia told herself grimly, irritated to find herself feeling uneasy beneath the highly intense, speculative gleam in the man's clear blue eyes.

'It is undoubtedly a great pleasure to meet you,' Lorenzo drawled, his lips twitching with amusement as he gazed at the attractive young woman.

Although she now appeared to be regarding him with a studiously closed, deadpan expression on her face, he'd been well aware, from the momentary tightening of her lips and the brief, fleeting glint of annoyance in those grey eyes, that she had no problem reading his mind.

'Nevertheless,' he continued smoothly, 'I'd be grateful if you could tell me why you're here.'

He was surprised by her reaction as she stared blankly at him for a moment, before giving a quick shake of her blonde head, clicking her teeth with annoyance as she crossed the room to hand him a small white card.

'I'm sorry. It looks as if there's been a bit of a slip-up, doesn't it?' She shrugged. 'I'd assumed that the agency would have left full details confirming my appointment, to be collected by you on your arrival here, at this hotel.'

'The agency?'

'James Riley, who runs Worldwide Security, is normally very efficient,' she quickly assured the man, who was frowning at her in some confusion. 'However, there's no need to worry,' she continued, looking quickly down at the slim gold watch on her wrist. 'I've personally seen to all the arrangements, and everything is now in place. So, if you're ready…?' She glanced over at his black dinner jacket, hanging over the back of a nearby chair. 'The chauffeur is waiting outside the back entrance, and…'

'*Just a minute!*' Lorenzo ground out, all trace of good humour swiftly vanishing from his face, as he gazed fixedly down at the white card in his hand. 'There *must* be some mistake!'

But, even as the baffled, incredulous note in his voice was still echoing loudly around the room, the truly awful, hideous truth was hitting him with all the force of a ten-ton truck.

'A mistake?' Antonia frowned. 'But the itinerary which I've been given of your engagements, here in London, plainly stated that you are due to attend the Albert Hall for a gala performance of...'

'*I* know where I'm going!' he snapped angrily. 'It's what *you* think you're doing here which concerns me.'

'I'm sorry, Signor Foscari. There seems to have been a complete breakdown in communications between yourself and Worldwide Security,' she told him quietly, hoping to take the heat out of what was looking like becoming a difficult situation. 'However, I have been appointed to act as your bodyguard...'

'What nonsense!'

'And I will be looking after you during your stay here, in Britain, to the very best of my ability,' she continued calmly, doing her best to ignore the man's stiff, rigid figure, and the baffled fury etched on his tanned face.

'But...but I was expecting a man! A Mr Tony Simpson,' Lorenzo ground out. 'Most definitely *not* a Miss Antonia Simpson. For heaven's sake—this is utterly ridiculous!' he added, his voice grating angrily around the room. 'I can't be expected to have a *woman* looking after me!'

Here we go again! Antonia told herself with grim resignation. It was exactly this sort of stupid anti-feminist, blind prejudice which had led her to form her own company, where she could call the shots, and not have to put up with such irritating male chauvinism.

However, it was obvious that she was going to have to take an immediate, firm grip on the situation. Especially as they were now in danger of running late, and upsetting her arrangements.

'How very clever of you to realise that I'm female,' she told him with a bland smile, quickly picking up his dinner *suit* jacket, and holding it towards him. 'Now, time is getting on. So, if you'll just put this on…'

'Don't you *dare* to try and patronise me!' he ground out through clenched teeth, before swearing violently under his breath. Mostly at himself—for automatically, without thought, taking the jacket from the woman and slipping it on over his broad shoulders.

'Let me tell you,' he continued angrily, 'that I absolutely refuse…'

'Yes, yes, of course you do,' she murmured soothingly, firmly propelling his tall figure out of the sitting room, and down the short hall towards the door. 'But we really must hurry.'

'*Santo cielo…!*' he exploded, suddenly digging in his heels and spinning around to face her. 'I am not going anywhere. And certainly *not* with you! *Capisce?*'

Antonia gazed at him coolly. 'Oh, sure. I understand all right—loud and clear!'

Used to dealing with difficult clients, she was well aware that, just at the moment, she had the upper hand. However, this man was clearly turning out to be both difficult and unpredictable. So there was no point in taking a hard line. Maybe she ought to take a more subtle approach to the problem…?

'To tell you the truth, Signor Foscari, I'm not a great opera buff,' she confided, with a brief shrug of her slim shoulders. 'So, if you don't mind disappointing your friends, by not bothering to turn up at the Albert Hall, that's OK by me. Quite frankly,' she added calmly, 'I'd be perfectly content to spend a quiet evening here, in the hotel. It's entirely up to you.'

Glaring down at her in baffled rage, his body rigid and

taut with fury, Lorenzo realised that the damn woman had him neatly boxed into a corner. Because of course he couldn't let his friends down. Certainly not at the last moment, and without any warning.

'Very well...' he growled. 'It seems that I have no choice in the matter. But I can assure you that I will be sorting out this totally ridiculous situation with your superiors first thing in the morning!'

'Very well,' she murmured, struggling to keep a straight face as she slipped past his stiff, angry figure to open the door, nodding to the man whom she'd stationed outside the suite, on her arrival at the hotel.

'You can tell the chauffeur that we're on our way,' she told him, waiting until she saw the guard issuing rapid instructions into his black handset, before turning back and holding the door open for Lorenzo. 'After you, Signor Foscari!'

'Thank you, Miss Simpson,' he grated through clenched teeth, throwing her a searing glance of pure, unadulterated loathing as he strode past her, and out into the corridor.

CHAPTER TWO

'I'M SORRY. This isn't exactly the smartest part of the hotel, but…'

'You're quite right—it most certainly is *not*!' Lorenzo agreed in a harsh, grating tone of voice, his tall figure rigid with outrage as he stared with disgust at the overflowing dustbins edging the pavement outside the rear service entrance.

'Yes, well…we'll soon have you out of here,' Antonia assured him quickly as the large black, chauffeur-driven limousine drew up beside them.

Just wait until I get my hands on James Riley! she told herself grimly, walking forward to open the passenger door of the limo. In fact, she was *definitely* going to enjoy having a few choice words with that gentleman! Because not only had James landed her with someone who was clearly the client from hell—but it looked as if he'd also managed to completely screw up the arrangements.

Even if he had informed Signor Foscari about the appointment of a bodyguard, James had clearly failed to provide the Italian with any other basic information regarding Close Protection. And why on earth he'd told the client that her name was Tony—a hangover from her childhood, which was only used nowadays amongst her family, and friends in the profession—she had no idea.

'If you'd like to take your seat in the vehicle…?' she murmured, holding the car door open and being careful not to make direct eye contact with Signor Foscari—who was clearly in a very tricky, nasty frame of mind.

'I do not recognise either this limousine or its driver,' he was saying, his voice hard and accusatory. 'Exactly *who* gave you the authority to dismiss my own car and chauffeur?'

She must at all costs remain non-confrontational, Antonia reminded herself, firmly suppressing a sudden urge to give the guy a good kick in the shins. The fact that he was becoming a first-class pain in the neck was obviously just her bad luck.

Unfortunately, and far more to the point, he appeared to be about as explosive as TNT—and equally unstable. So, the sooner she managed to take the steam out of the situation the better.

'It's merely the usual, standard procedure—all of which is designed to ensure your complete safety,' she told him quietly, deliberately keeping her voice empty of all expression, with her gaze firmly fixed on a point just below his tightly clenched jaw.

'My safety?' Lorenzo gave a snort of derision. 'I was perfectly safe until the arrival of you, and this…this *gorilla*!' he added, turning to glare at the tall, thick-set guard standing behind him. His fury increased as the large man merely responded to the insult with a cheerful grin.

'I can assure you that Martin is a very experienced, highly trained operative,' Antonia retorted, relieved to note that her colleague wasn't taking any notice of the Italian's clear loss of temper.

In fact, when swiftly escorting the grim-faced Signor Foscari along the hotel corridor, and down the back service stairs, Martin had murmured in her ear, 'You'd better watch it, Tony. This guy looks as if he's on a *very* short fuse!'

'Tell me about it!' she'd muttered, grateful for the solid, reliable back-up of the ex-paratrooper, with whom she'd worked closely over the years.

However, if they didn't get a move on, Signor Foscari was going to be late for the opera. So, she must somehow find a way of persuading this extremely difficult man to get into the limousine.

'You really have no need to worry about your new chauffeur,' she assured him firmly. 'Not only is he fully conversant with all aspects of close protection, but should there be an emergency he would immediately be able to...'

Lorenzo Foscari's harsh bark of sardonic laughter cut sharply across her words.

'Kindly spare me the sales pitch, Miss Simpson!' he snapped curtly. Glaring down at her for a few tense moments, he eventually gave a shrug of his broad shoulders, before taking a few steps forward and entering the car.

Antonia gave a heavy sigh of relief. She didn't like admitting the fact, of course. But, just for a few seconds, she'd found herself feeling distinctly nervous. Which was, of course, totally ridiculous. Especially as she was used to handling far tougher, rougher-looking men than Lorenzo Foscari.

Waiting until Martin had taken his place in the front of the vehicle beside the driver, she took a deep breath before joining her client in the rear of the limousine.

Taking the radio receiver out of her handbag, she alerted the back-up car, waiting around the corner in Grosvenor Crescent, that they were about to leave, before giving the go-ahead to her own driver.

Preoccupied in making sure that her arrangements went smoothly, she gradually realised that Signor Foscari had so far remained remarkably silent.

Long may it last! Antonia told herself, glancing cautiously through her eyelashes at the profile of the tall, dark figure sitting at the far end of the wide leather seat.

The dying rays of the summer sun were casting a rosy glow over the tanned, hawk-like features of the man, who was staring straight ahead and was clearly buried deep in thought. From the enigmatic, inscrutable expression on his face, it was impossible for her to guess what was going through his mind. She could only hope that he'd begun to calm down, and regard the whole situation in a more reasonable frame of mind. But, the way her luck was going at the moment, he was just as likely to suddenly erupt, once again, in a violent storm of rage and fury.

Her thoughts were interrupted by the squawks issuing from the small black receiver in her hand.

'It's a nuisance, but it can't be helped,' she said, after listening to the message being relayed by the car in front. 'I suggest that you take the next right turn, and we'll go through the park, OK?' she added, waiting until she'd received an acknowledgement of her instructions before turning to face Lorenzo.

'There seems to be a bit of a traffic jam ahead. So we're now making a slight detour through Hyde Park.'

'Is that likely to delay my arrival at the Albert Hall?' he asked quietly.

'No.' She shook her head, relieved to discover that her client now appeared to have calmed down. 'We should still be in plenty of time for you to have a drink with your friends, before taking your seat for the opera.'

'I'm glad to hear it!' he murmured, giving her a surprisingly friendly grin, before querying the system she was using to communicate with her operatives.

'I can understand the reasons why you need to be in touch with the vehicle in front of us. But I fail to see why, when you want to say something to our chauffeur, you cannot just slide apart that partition,' he added, nodding towards the glass barrier between themselves and the men in front.

'While you have a bodyguard in here with you, that glass partition is always kept firmly closed,' she told him. 'It's made of bullet-proof glass—as are all the other windows in this vehicle. So, if anything should happen to the driver…'

'Like getting shot?'

'Well…er…something along those lines,' she murmured, before adding quickly, 'Although that's *very* unlikely, of course. I mean, there's no need for you to worry about details like that.'

'Oh, I'm not at all worried, Miss Simpson,' he drawled, turning his dark head to give her a warm, charming smile. 'To tell you the truth,' he added, 'I've never believed that these so-called threats against my life were anything other than total nonsense.'

'Once someone *has* issued threats, there's always a risk that they will try and carry them out,' she pointed out, finding it surprisingly hard to resist the almost beguiling warmth and charm of the man sitting beside her. Not to mention that low, positively toe-curling, sexy Italian accent of his—which appeared to be having a very strange effect on her whole nervous system.

'You are, of course, quite right,' he agreed with a heavy sigh. 'In fact…' he hesitated for a moment '…I now realise that I was, perhaps, guilty of behaving badly, back at the hotel. I was, of course, obviously tired…possibly the effect of jet lag…? You know how it is?' he added, with a casual shrug of his broad shoulders.

'Yes, well…'

'Which is why, my dear Miss Simpson, I do hope that you will find it in your heart to forgive my lapse of bad manners?'

Phew! Talk about a volte face! Antonia told herself, almost reeling from the devastating impact of yet another warmly caressing, almost intimate smile.

Well! At least one thing was now as clear as daylight. This guy hadn't just decided to be reasonable—he was obviously intent on mounting a full-scale charm offensive! And unfortunately, if the way she was suddenly having difficulty with her breathing, was anything to go by, it was proving highly effective.

'I quite understand. There's no need to apologise,' she muttered, making an effort to pull herself together.

Which was surprisingly difficult. Especially as her mind,

for some extraordinary reason, seemed to be temporarily out of order. But maybe that had something to do with the highly-disturbing sensual atmosphere which seemed to be rapidly filling the confined space of the vehicle.

Trying to ignore the tall, dark figure sitting beside her, Antonia tried to work out what the damned man was up to. Because there was definitely no 'perhaps' about his bad behaviour back at the hotel. He'd been an absolute *swine*—and well he knew it!

Her thoughts were sharply interrupted as the car in front abruptly slammed on its brakes. Leaning forward in her seat, she saw that its progress was being impeded by a group of young teenagers on roller-blades.

Swiftly scanning the area of the park through which they were travelling—which contained only a few courting couples, either sitting on the grass or strolling quietly amongst the trees—she quickly lifted her handset.

'Relax…the kids are just having a bit of fun, and enjoying themselves. Ignore them—they'll soon get bored and leave us alone,' she instructed, almost envying the ability of the youths to control their thin steel blades as they swooped and dived between the two vehicles.

Her quick assessment of the situation proved to be correct, with the teenagers quickly growing tired of the game, and racing off down the road in search of new victims.

As the two limousines resumed their journey, Antonia leaned back in her seat, her eyes following the young kids as she wondered if she was too old—or, possibly, far too sensible—to take up the sport herself.

A silent spectator to the brief interruption of their progress, Lorenzo couldn't prevent his lips twitching with amusement, having no problem in accurately guessing the thoughts going through her mind.

And why not? he mused. With her tall, athletic figure, she would undoubtedly master the art of roller-blading—just as smoothly and efficiently as she appeared to do everything else.

As soon as he'd entered this limousine, a few moments' reflection had led him to realise that losing his temper with this imperturbable woman had achieved precisely nothing. However, he hadn't climbed swiftly up the corporate ladder of the business world without learning a thing or two, he'd reminded himself grimly. And one of the chief lessons had been the need for flexibility.

Which was precisely why he'd swiftly come to the conclusion that, of all the options open to him, an attempt to drown the highly irritating young woman in honey might prove to be a better choice of tactics.

However, despite her apparent agreement to forget and forgive his loss of temper, back at the hotel, he'd been well aware of the cautious, wary glint in her smoky-grey eyes.

So...although he couldn't recall ever having a problem in charming a woman out of her mind, it didn't look as if he'd even got to first base with Miss Antonia Simpson.

Unfortunately, he knew absolutely nothing about her. Which placed him at a considerable disadvantage. Because, when dealing with a business opponent, it was information on the other man's background, and his likely response to any pressure, which had always proved an invaluable tool in any negotiation.

In the present case, he had nothing to go on. No idea of what made this woman 'tick'. Nor, indeed, what on earth had persuaded her to take up such an extraordinarily bizarre occupation.

As the limousine began gathering speed, and they continued their progress through Hyde Park, Lorenzo leaned back in his seat, giving him a better view of the tall, slim figure of the blonde sitting beside him.

She was definitely *not* his type, he told himself firmly. He had never been attracted to this sort of arrogant, domineering female, who clearly considered herself the equal of any man.

In fact, almost without exception, his girlfriends had always been dark, slender and petite, with an enchanting air of delicate fragility. And, while it was true that some had been tiresome—either totally self-absorbed, or given to amazing displays of temperament—they had *never*, under *any* circumstances, made the mistake of trying to push him around. Nor would they have dreamed of trying to tell him what he could and could not do!

On the other hand…if he hadn't been so annoyed with her, he might be prepared to admit that Antonia Simpson was a highly attractive, good-looking woman. He'd certainly thought so when she'd first marched into his suite, earlier this evening.

Allowing his gaze to sweep over the firm breasts, clearly outlined as she raised a hand to tuck a lock of hair behind her ear, and the short skirt of her dress, displaying long, slim legs encased in sheer black silk stockings, merely confirmed his first impression.

However, by the time their vehicle was finally approaching the Albert Hall, Lorenzo had abruptly changed his mind again.

Neither the use of as much charm as he could summon up under the circumstances nor—as a desperate last resort—his frank offer of bribery and corruption had in any way managed to dent the cool self-possession of this extraordinary young woman.

'Relax, Signor Foscari!' she'd told him with a wide, unusually enchanting smile, which suddenly had the effect of making her appear almost beautiful. 'Believe me, I *really* appreciate that Italian charm of yours! But unfortunately trying to sweet-talk me into abandoning the job I've been hired to do is a pure waste of your time.

'And I'm afraid that offering me a great deal of money to get out of your life won't work either,' she'd added, with another broad, ironic grin. 'Unfortunately, I have a contract with your insurance company. And, until *they* dismiss me, I'm afraid that you and I will just have to put up with one another. *Capisce?*'

He probably deserved that last, verbal slap in the face, Lorenzo told himself grimly. And, while he might actively dislike the girl sitting next to him, he had to admit that she was proving to be a quite impressive adversary.

However, the situation in which he found himself was still utterly intolerable. And he certainly had *no* intention of putting up with her appointment—or of allowing himself to be swayed by that enchanting smile—one moment longer than he had to.

But even as he rallied his forces—pointing out that he could not gain admittance to the concert hall without a ticket, which he'd unfortunately left behind in his hotel room—the damned woman merely gave a brief shrug of her slim shoulders.

'There's no problem. I picked it up from the hall table before we left your suite,' she said, clearly enjoying his discomfiture as she removed the ticket from her handbag.

'And what about you?' he demanded, through gritted teeth, as their vehicle drew to a halt outside the concert hall. 'Exactly how are *you* planning to spend the evening? Standing outside my friends' box for three hours, until the end of the performance, doesn't sound much fun.'

'I'm not being paid a great deal of money just to have fun,' she retorted dismissively, before opening the car door, and he found himself being swiftly escorted inside the large dome of the Albert Hall.

'Hi, there! We were just beginning to wonder if you'd make it here tonight,' Giles Harding called out, hurrying through the crowd towards him.

'O, ye of little faith.' Lorenzo grinned at his old friend, before turning to greet Giles's wife, Susie Harding.

Busy chatting to Susie, and catching up with their family's news, he just about managed to temporarily forget

Antonia. However, if he'd hoped to have seen the last of her—for a few hours, at least—he was doomed to disappointment.

'Aha! You lucky dog! I might have known that you'd turn up with a gorgeous girlfriend in tow,' Giles murmured with a grin, giving him a sharp dig in the ribs as he spotted the tall girl standing behind the tall Italian.

'I'm so glad you could join us,' Giles said, taking her arm with a beaming smile, before Lorenzo had a chance to explain that Miss Simpson was most definitely *not* his girlfriend.

'There's no problem with seats, since two of our guests had to cancel at the last minute,' Giles added, handing her a drink, before quickly introducing her to his wife.

Chatting idly with his friends' guests—a rather boring banker and his wife—amidst the noise of loud voices and laughter in the large bar, Lorenzo realised that there was virtually nothing he could do about the situation.

It placed him in an awkward position, of course. On the other hand, he certainly didn't want to have to go into long, tedious explanations of why he apparently needed protection. Especially as he was almost certain that his old friends would find the highly embarrassing, humiliating fact that he was being forced to put up with a *female* bodyguard absolutely hilarious.

Initially surprised to find herself being greeted as his girlfriend, Antonia had glanced enquiringly at Lorenzo, indicating her willingness to go along with the scenario.

In her job, she'd frequently been called upon to act the part of a devoted wife or loving fiancée—especially when engaged in undercover work, such as trailing a suspect. So assuming the role of Lorenzo's girlfriend wasn't likely to be too difficult.

And maybe…maybe, if he'd made even the slightest effort to act his part, she might not have lost her temper with the foul man. But, after clearly deciding to let Giles Harding believe that she was his latest popsy, Lorenzo had proceeded to totally ignore her, turning his back and chatting to his friends and their guests as if he'd never even heard of her existence.

Goodness knows, she'd already had to put up with quite enough of his nonsense this evening. Besides, she wasn't stupid. She could easily understand why he hadn't corrected his friend's mistake. But there was no excuse for him to behave in such a boorish fashion.

In fact, it was the way he was trying to have his cake—and eat it too—which finally tipped her over the edge.

As the bell rang, signalling that the performance was about to start, and the crowd began moving out of the bar towards the auditorium, she adroitly moved up behind Lorenzo's tall figure, before casually slipping her arm through his.

'Sweetie! You weren't thinking of leaving me behind, were you?' she exclaimed with a light ripple of laughter, before raising her head to give him a wide, beaming smile.

Rewarded by the sudden tensing of his tall body, and the brief look of horror flickering over his handsome, tanned face, Antonia turned to smile at the Hardings and their guests.

'I'm so pleased that darling Lorenzo brought me here tonight. I've been longing to see this opera for ages. Such a treat!' she told them, with another warm, happy smile, maintaining a firm grip on his arm as they entered the box.

Swiftly glancing around the red plush interior, which hadn't changed since the days of Queen Victoria, Antonia quickly identified the perfect position for her client. Letting go of Lorenzo's arm, she casually edged a nearby chair into a position which would shield him from any possible assassin in the audience—while still allowing him a good sight of the large stage below.

'Why don't you sit here, darling?' she murmured with a soft, winsome smile.

'No, thank you,' he retorted through gritted teeth, clearly

furious at having to maintain a fixed, pleasant expression on his face, solely for the benefit of his hosts and their guests. 'I'm sure one of the other ladies would prefer to...'

'Don't be silly, darling—I insist that *you* sit there,' she told him firmly, accompanying her words with another simpering, entirely false smile. A smile which had those present gazing indulgently at what they, quite mistakenly, assumed to be a loving couple.

As Lorenzo stood glaring down at her, his body taut and rigid with anger at finding himself totally outmanoeuvred, she thought for one, wild moment that he might throw caution to the winds and indulge in a spectacular loss of temper. However, after what appeared to be a massive inner struggle, he finally managed to bring himself under control.

'*Why don't you go to hell!*' he ground out savagely under his breath as, very reluctantly, he lowered himself into the chair.

'Only if *you* lead the way, *sweetie*!' she retorted with a grin, before seating herself just behind his tall figure.

As the house lights dimmed and the orchestra began playing the overture, Lorenzo leaned back in his comfortable red plush seat, a bland expression on his face—and murder in his heart!

He'd never, in the whole of his life, been tempted to even *think* of using violence of any kind against a woman. Which made it all the more shocking to now find himself actively contemplating—with *considerable* pleasure!—the untimely demise of Miss Antonia Simpson.

Right from the moment that bossy, thoroughly irritating young woman had marched so confidently into his hotel suite, earlier this evening, he'd suspected that she was likely to be up to no good. And how right he'd been. Because the brazen hussy had turned out to be nothing but trouble, with a capital T!

What had he ever done to deserve such a fate? Lorenzo

asked himself grimly as, on the stage below the box, the chorus and orchestra wound themselves up for the grand entrance of Otello—returning home to Venice in triumph, after soundly beating the Turkish Navy.

Living most of the year in Milan, he'd regularly visited La Scala—in his opinion, the greatest opera house in the world. And he had, of course, seen many productions of Verdi's tragic opera, based on the play *Othello*, by William Shakespeare.

But only now did it occur to him that the story of a man driven out of his mind by external forces and culminating in his murder of his wife, Desdemona, seemed strangely appropriate to his own current predicament.

Don't be ridiculous! It's time you got a grip on the situation! Lorenzo lectured himself sternly.

The fact that Antonia Simpson had managed to have everything her own way, so far, was no reason to allow her to push him around for the foreseeable future. Which meant that the sooner he got his act together the better.

Oh, yes! It was about time he taught that domineering, high-handed, so-called 'bodyguard' of his a lesson which she wouldn't forget in a hurry.

For her part, and greatly to her surprise, Antonia found herself enjoying the opera. In fact, she would have found it totally absorbing if she hadn't been required to be fully alert on behalf of Lorenzo Foscari.

This was *definitely* the last job she'd ever take on for that ratfink James Riley. Goodness knows, she'd looked after some tiresome people in the past. But this oh, so macho Italian—who clearly should have been strangled at birth—just about took the biscuit!

All the same, maybe it hadn't been *too* clever of her to try and score a few points off the swine just now, she told herself. Recalling her impression, earlier in the evening, that he was as tricky and unpredictable as dynamite, she realised it might possibly have been a mistake to have momentarily lost her own temper—simply because she'd considered him guilty of bad manners.

Because, however tempting it might have been to cut the man down to size, it definitely wasn't the response expected from an experienced and highly capable bodyguard.

She was a professional, Antonia reminded herself firmly. Which was why, despite all provocation, she *must* strive to maintain an air of cool, calm efficiency and detachment remaining totally aloof and objective at all times. It also meant, she told herself grimly, that she was going to have to find some way of coping with this extraordinarily difficult man.

Unfortunately, it was becoming clear that Lorenzo Foscari wasn't just your ordinary, run-of-the-mill client.

He was, of course, extremely arrogant and overbearing. Not to mention his quite extraordinary, old-fashioned, chauvinistic attitude to women. The way he'd gone completely ballistic, at the appointment of a female bodyguard was totally ridiculous in this day and age.

On the other hand…well…there was no denying the fact that he did possess a disturbing aura of rampant sex appeal. And, when he wasn't busy losing his temper, he appeared to have been born with an equally large quota of overwhelming, almost mesmerising charm. Charm which he was quite prepared to use as a weapon, she reminded herself sharply, recalling his unscrupulous attempts to undermine her contract with his insurance company.

So, the fact that the man was a high-octane, lethal mixture of barely leashed force and aggression, coupled with an almost irresistible warmth and attraction, meant that he wasn't just a difficult man, but also a highly complex one. There was no doubt that she was going to have to keep her wits about her, at all times, Antonia told herself with a heavy sigh. There was no way she'd be able to relax her guard on *this* job! A conclusion that was reinforced as she turned to view the man sitting on her left, just slightly in front of her own chair.

Despite the dim light within the box, and with only his sharply etched profile in view, one didn't need a very high IQ to read Lorenzo Foscari's body language. And the message it conveyed was not a happy one.

The muscle beating furiously in his tightly clenched jaw, and the rigidly tense, broad shoulders beneath his expensive black dinner jacket provided plenty of evidence that the guy was still *very* angry. Maybe the wonderful music would help him to calm down?

Rarely attending concerts in the Albert Hall, Antonia had forgotten that the larger boxes surrounding the auditorium also contained a small, individual area at the back—designed for the service of food and drink during the interval.

Since Giles and Susie Harding had been kind enough to include her in their party, she felt the least she could do when the curtain came down for the interval, to give Susie a hand with the light supper—which the older woman had brought with her in a large picnic hamper.

'I've kept it very simple,' Susie told her, removing various plates from the wicker basket. 'Just champagne, smoked salmon sandwiches and, to finish the meal, some strawberries and cream.'

'It sounds absolutely delicious—and not at all simple!' Antonia said with a slight laugh as the older woman delved into the hamper to extract some icy cold bottles of champagne.

'Well...I really meant that it took the minimum of effort. Because all I had to do was to make the sandwiches,' Susie explained with a grin, before handing the champagne to her husband, with a brisk instruction to make sure that everyone had enough to drink.

'So, tell me,' Susie enquired as she tipped the strawberries into a large bowl, 'have you known Lorenzo for long?'

'No. We...er...we only met fairly recently,' Antonia murmured, glancing quickly across the room to where Lorenzo appeared to be deep in conversation with the stuffy banker.

'He and Giles were at school together, so dear Lorenzo is one of our oldest friends,' Susie explained. 'He's gorgeous, isn't he? So attractive, so charming...and *so* rich. An absolutely *lethal* combination!' she added with a grin.

Wondering whether she was being warned off, Antonia was just about to reassure her hostess that she and Lorenzo were definitely *not* interested in one another, when Susie quickly shook her head.

'Oh, no—don't get me wrong. Giles and I are absolutely delighted that Lorenzo has brought you along here tonight,' she said, placing the sandwiches on some small plates for distribution amongst the guests. 'We reckon that it's about time he stopped living life in the fast lane, and settled down with a wife—and lots of *bambini* too, of course!' Susie added with a grin. 'So, if he has finally managed to dump that awful woman, Gina Lombardi, I couldn't be more happy! In fact,' she confided with a wink, 'Giles and I reckon that you and Lorenzo are just made for each other!'

This is getting to be a very heavy scene! Antonia told herself, giving the other woman a brief, noncommittal smile.

Deliberately trying to score a few points off the foul man was one thing. But Giles and Susie were obviously a very nice couple. So she really didn't like the idea of trying to deliberately deceive or fool them into believing that she was romantically involved with Lorenzo.

'To tell you the truth, Susie, as far as Lorenzo and I are concerned...' She paused, carefully choosing her words as she continued, 'Well, the fact is...'

'The fact is...we're simply mad with each other!' Lorenzo's deep voice completed the sentence, from just behind her left shoulder.

Startled by his sudden appearance, Antonia found herself taken utterly by surprise as he quickly slipped an arm about her waist, before firmly clasping her to the side of his strong body.

'No—you idiot!' Susie laughingly told him. 'The correct expression is not mad *with* but mad *about* each other.'

'Ah, yes—I must improve my use of the English language,' he agreed smoothly. 'However, darling Antonia knows *exactly* how I feel about her. Isn't that right, *sweetie*?'

Damn right I do! she told herself grimly, wondering how he'd managed to creep up on her so quickly and silently? She must be slipping, because it wasn't like her to be taken by surprise like this.

Unfortunately, unless she was prepared to cause a scene, there was nothing she could do to free herself from the hard, muscular strength of the arm which was keeping her so tightly pinned against his tall figure.

'I'm *so* lucky to have Antonia looking after me. We have such a *close* relationship,' Lorenzo was telling his hostess. 'Mmm…strawberries! How delicious. They're my favourite fruit,' he added, reaching forward to pick a very large, succulent berry from the bowl as Antonia turned her head to glare up at him.

'You're fond of them too, aren't you, *darling*?' he murmured, smiling so warmly and tenderly down at the girl clasped to his side that Susie found herself giving a small sigh of pure envy.

'Yes, they're very nice,' Antonia muttered, still feeling slightly confused and thrown off balance by the way Lorenzo was suddenly playing the part of her red-hot lover. Especially as she was only too well aware of the chilly, icy cold gleam in the eyes staring down into her own.

'However, I was just telling Susie that…*Whaa-aa*…!' she gasped as Lorenzo adroitly popped the large strawberry into her mouth, rendering her temporarily speechless.

'Mmm…yes, they clearly *are* delicious!' he murmured, his lips twitching with sardonic laughter as he viewed

Antonia's cheeks bulging while she struggled to cope with a huge mouthful of juicy red fruit.

'Would you like some more, darling?' he added, maintaining the firm grip of his arm about her body as he reached forward to choose another large fruit from the bowl.

'*Nuh!*' Antonia mumbled helplessly, giving a quick shake of her head, and glaring up at him with utter loathing.

'Isn't she amusing?' Lorenzo exclaimed as Antonia gulped, finally managing to swallow the huge strawberry. And then, with Susie looking on and beaming at what she clearly regarded as a happy couple, he lowered his dark head as if about to kiss his new girlfriend's cheek.

But, even as she instinctively flinched, quickly turning her head away from him, she realised that he'd never had any intention of kissing her. Far from it.

Pressing his lips to her ear, he whispered savagely, 'Let that be a lesson, sweetie! *Never* make the mistake of trying to mess around with me, again—or you'll be *very* sorry! OK?'

He waited until she gave a slight nod before loosening his grip on her waist and strolling off to have a word with Giles Harding.

'You're so lucky!' Susie sighed deeply, before turning away to hand small plates of sandwiches to the banker and his wife.

Oh, yeah? Antonia's eyes narrowed with baffled rage and fury as she stared at Lorenzo, who'd clearly regained his good humour as she saw him laughing at something his host was saying. If she ever got the chance for revenge, she promised herself grimly, that arrogant swine was *definitely* going to regret, what he'd just done!

Following the performance, the short journey back to the hotel was conducted in silence. Which was mainly due to the fact that Antonia, after battling to control her anger during the last act of the opera, was still trying to simmer down and pull herself together.

She knew that she'd been originally in the wrong, and so might have been prepared to call it quits, and do her best to forget the incident, if Lorenzo Foscari hadn't been so cheerful. Although, what he had to be so happy about was absolutely beyond her. However, it looked as if putting her down had done his own temper a power of good, she told herself sourly.

Glancing through her eyelashes at the hawk-like profile of the man sitting beside her, she noted that he was still quietly humming a tune from the opera, while taking an interest in the brilliantly lit shop windows of Knightsbridge.

After directing the car to the rear of the hotel, and arranging which guards could be released and which should stay on duty, Antonia accompanied Lorenzo up the back stairs towards his suite.

She had to calm down, she told herself firmly. If Lorenzo Foscari wanted to play stupid games—that was entirely up to him. She, for her part, must remain totally calm and professional at all times.

'Well…that was a *very* interesting evening,' he drawled as they entered the suite. 'Can I fix you a drink?' he added, walking across the carpet to a bar, in a far corner of the large sitting room.

'No, thank you. I never drink when on duty.'

'Ah, yes…I've been thinking about your duties as my *personal* bodyguard,' he murmured, pouring himself a stiff whisky, before turning around to give her a broad smile. 'And I came to one or two interesting conclusions.'

'Oh, yes?' Antonia eyed him warily. She was beginning to realise that when Lorenzo Foscari turned on the charm he generally had some devious objective in mind.

He shrugged. 'We both know that I was less than pleased to find myself landed with a bodyguard. Nor was I too happy to discover that she was female. Not that I have anything against women, of course...'

'You could have fooled me!'

'It's just that I foresaw certain...er...difficulties in such an appointment,' he continued, clearly choosing to ignore her interjection. 'However, after giving the situation much thought, I suddenly realised that those ''difficulties'' were, in fact, a positive bonus!'

She frowned. 'Sorry—I don't have a clue what you're talking about.'

'I'm talking about the fact that, as my bodyguard, you are concerned with the *close* and *personal* protection of my body,' he drawled smoothly, walking slowly over to where she was standing by the doorway.

'So?'

'You have, I understand, been hired to guard my body for twenty-four hours a day?'

'Yes, technically speaking, I suppose I have. But...'

'Well, there you are!' He grinned wolfishly down at her. 'I suddenly realised that it would be churlish, to say the least, to turn down the opportunity of having *you*, my dear Antonia, closely guarding my body through the night.'

She stared at him in amazement for a moment, before being struck by the utterly ridiculous aspect of the situation.

'You *must* be joking!' she laughed.

'Oh, no—not at all,' he murmured, his eyes gleaming beneath their heavy lids. 'In fact, I'm beginning to find the idea of us spending the night together quite an enchanting prospect. Tell me...on which side of the bed do you prefer to sleep?'

'Don't be ridiculous!' she snapped.

Antonia was almost certain that he was just winding her up. But she was determined to put this guy straight about the relationship between a bodyguard and their client. Who did he think she was? Some kind of Mata Hari?

'Your insurance company has hired me to act as your

personal bodyguard,' she told him firmly. 'And yes, I do have the overall responsibility of making sure that you have close, adequate protection around the clock. But…'

'Wonderful!' he exclaimed with another wolf-like grin. 'I don't wear pyjamas, of course. But, I'm sure a real professional, such as yourself, has a great line in sexy nightdresses, hmm?'

'Oh—*come on*! Are you completely incapable of listening to a word I've been saying?' she demanded irritably, refusing to be intimidated by the tall, dark figure now looming over her. 'Believe me, I have absolutely *no* intention of spending the night here, in your suite.'

'What? Are you intending to welsh on the deal?' he queried with mock indignation. 'That is disgraceful! I shall certainly report this dereliction of duty to your superiors.'

'Ha-ha—very funny!' she ground out sarcastically. 'However, if you want to check, you'll find that there is already a guard stationed outside in the corridor,' she added curtly. 'He, working together with a colleague, will make absolutely certain that you are not disturbed during the night.'

'And you?

'I will be in the suite adjacent to this one—with the door *firmly* locked!' she retorted swiftly. 'Although why you seem to think that I'd want to share your bed is completely beyond me!' she added with a shrill, high-pitched laugh. '*You* may think that you're totally irresistible, but, quite frankly, *sweetie*, I'm not *that* desperate!'

He took a step forward, his expression suddenly hard and threatening.

'Be careful, Antonia!' he growled. 'As you undoubtedly realised, I was merely enjoying a joke with you. However, I really don't care to be talked to in such a disrespectful manner.'

'Tough!' she retorted, suddenly deciding that she'd had quite enough of this unbelievably tiresome Italian for one day.

'Although, believe me, if I *was* in frantic need of a man,' she added with another, high-pitched laugh, 'I sure as hell wouldn't waste any time chasing after an uptight male chauvinist such as yourself!'

In the dead silence which followed, she was aware of Lorenzo Foscari's quick, sharp inhalation of breath, a dark flush sweeping over his cheeks.

'Oh, really?' he muttered savagely. His blue eyes, like chips of tungsten steel, bore down into hers as his hands came down on her shoulders.

'OK—let's cool it, huh?' she muttered, quickly pulling herself together. What on earth was she doing, quarrelling with a client like this? Even if the gentleman concerned was enough to try the patience of a saint, her behaviour was well out of order.

But, as Antonia discovered for the second time that evening, she was guilty of seriously underestimating an opponent.

Despite always priding herself on her quick reactions, she realised that she'd been completely outclassed and outgunned, as Lorenzo suddenly moved at what seemed to be the speed of light. A nanosecond later, she found herself firmly clasped by one steely, unyielding arm to his hard, tall body, while he placed his other hand firmly beneath her chin.

Tilting her face up towards him, she barely had time to become aware of his blue eyes glittering down at her before his dark head was descending swiftly towards her—his mouth possessing her lips in a kiss of devastating intensity.

CHAPTER THREE

SHOCKED and stunned by the totally unexpected swiftness of Lorenzo's action, Antonia took a second or two to begin trying to struggle free from his strong arms.

Bitterly ashamed of being such an idiot, and having stupidly underestimated both this man's strength and his likely speed of movement, she gradually realised that the hand firmly placed on her back was now beginning to slide slowly and seductively down over her body.

The hardening muscles of his strong thighs, clasped so tightly to her own, suddenly prompted a fierce clench of sexual awareness deep in the pit of her stomach, which left her feeling weak and trembling.

She had no idea of what was happening to her. But it was clear that they were now both in a high state of arousal. As he ruthlessly forced her lips apart, the moistly erotic heat of his tongue, savagely exploring the sweet, inner softness of her mouth, was driving her almost wild with excitement.

As if he sensed her bewilderment and confusion, her inability to cope with the sudden flash-flood of hot desire scorching through her veins, his mouth relaxed its hard pressure as his hands travelled slowly and erotically over the soft curves of her body. She was dimly conscious of the rapid, deep thudding of his heartbeat, of her nostrils filled with the musky scent of his cologne, and the warmth of his mouth, now moving softly and seductively over her quivering lips.

It was as if time was standing still and she, hopelessly trapped by her own emotions, was utterly powerless. She seemed to have no choice, but to respond to the increasingly fiery tide of sensual excitement and sheer naked lust pounding and rampaging through her trembling body.

Only when she became aware that he was unzipping her dress, her bare flesh quivering with delight beneath the soft, warm touch of the fingers trailing down her spine to undo her bra strap, did harsh reality begin to break through the thick mist of overwhelming desire clouding her mind.

Oh, my God...what on earth was she doing? This...this man was a client, for heaven's sake!

It seemed to take the most enormous effort. But at last she managed to force herself to make a serious, determined attempt to break out of his embrace. Struggling free, she raised her hands to push him away as, at the same time, she threw herself sharply backwards. Only to have the breath almost knocked out of her trembling, shaking body as her spine jarred painfully up against the wall by the door.

'*Ouch!*' she gasped, wincing as she fought to regain her breath for a moment.

He frowned, taking a step forward. 'Are you all right?'

'Keep away from me!' she ground out, turning away to frantically adjust her bra and zip up her dress, before swiftly turning back to confront the man, standing only a foot or so away from her shaken figure.

'What...what do you think you were doing?' she demanded, glaring at Lorenzo Foscari, who was now gazing enigmatically down at her through his half-closed, heavy eyelids.

But, as her breathless voice seemed to echo around the large room, the foul man merely gave a low rumble of sardonic laughter.

'I think you have a slight problem with your English grammar,' he drawled coolly. 'Surely, that question should have been phrased "What do *we* think *we've been* doing"?'

'Singular or plural—who cares?' she snapped, not only very angry with him, but also raging at her own stupidity, in having responded so blindly and helplessly to this man's overwhelming attraction.

'And I note that you haven't even had the grace to apologise for your *disgusting* behaviour!' she added, almost beside herself with fury. Because, while she was still having trouble trying to pull herself together, the rotten man was coolly standing there without a hair out of place.

'Apologise?' He raised a dark, quizzical eyebrow. 'My dear Antonia, why on earth should I apologise for that delightful kiss? In fact, I was entranced by your enthusiastic response to my embrace. Are you quite sure, that you don't want to guard my body, tonight?'

'Oh—*shut up!*' she ground out through clenched teeth, having no problem in noting that his blue eyes were gleaming with mockery and laughter. However, there was clearly no point in prolonging this embarrassing scene one minute longer than she had to.

'I'm now going to walk out of here,' she told him coldly as she turned to leave the room. 'And, if I do not receive your unreserved apology by nine o'clock tomorrow morning I will regard our contract as having been terminated.'

Unfortunately, what should have been a dignified exit was spoiled as, for some unaccountable reason, her coordination seemed to have been shot to pieces.

Fumbling with the handle, as she struggled to open the door leading out of the room, she could feel her face burning with shame and humiliation at the low rumble of his sardonic laughter—which was still echoing loudly in her ears long after she'd slammed the front door of his suite of rooms behind her.

Antonia gave a heavy sigh. It was no good. After spending two hours tossing and turning in the darkness of her luxurious bedroom, it was clearly time she gave up the unequal fight to seek oblivion in sleep.

After turning over to switch on her bedroom light, she

threw back the bedclothes before slipping on a light dressing gown and padding barefoot across the thick-pile carpet towards the large sitting room of the suite—a mirror image of that occupied by her client next door.

No one could accuse his insurance company of being cheeseparing, she thought, gazing around the large room as she lifted the phone to order a large pot of soothing tea.

Lorenzo Foscari must be a very important client if they were prepared to spend this sort of money on a bedroom suite for his bodyguard. In fact, the only difference between her suite and Lorenzo's was that her sitting room was now fitted out like an office, designed for use as a communications centre during daylight hours.

Since she *was* still wide awake at this unearthly hour, it might be a good idea to check the situation with one of the guards whom she'd stationed outside Lorenzo's suite.

'No problems, Tony,' the man confirmed, his voice sounding tinny and ghost-like through the ear-piece of her walkie-talkie. 'It's as quiet as the grave out here.'

'I'm glad to hear it. Oh, by the way,' she added quickly, 'I've just ordered a pot of tea from Room Service. So a waiter will be coming along the corridor any minute now. OK?'

'Yeah, no problem. But you'd better try and get some sleep,' he warned her. 'A lack of shut-eye isn't good news in our business.'

'Tell me about it!' she muttered grimly, before switching off her handset.

Her colleague had been quite right, Antonia told herself some time later as she poured herself a cup of hot, sweet tea.

Spending a large part of the night wide awake was definitely a bad move. Especially for someone who was expected to be bright-eyed, bushy-tailed and fully alert the following day. In fact, she'd never before had a problem in immediately falling asleep, just as soon as her head hit the pillow.

But then, she reminded herself with a heavy sigh, she'd *never* experienced such difficulties with a client as she had with Lorenzo Foscari. And it was deeply galling to realise that most of the problems had been her own stupid fault.

There was no point in trying to fool herself. It was plain that not only had she behaved in a totally amateurish, unprofessional manner, but she'd also made just about every mistake in the book.

For instance, it had been incredibly foolish of her to even think of deliberately taunting the man. Especially as she already knew that he was both explosive and unpredictable. And then to have allowed herself to be provoked into bluntly telling him where to get off had been the height of folly.

What made the situation *far* worse was the fact that if she'd *really* tried Antonia knew that she could have broken free of his embrace. Despite the fact that Lorenzo was clearly very fit and agile, there was no way he could have kept her imprisoned in his arms for very long. Not if she'd been *truly* determined to escape.

But, despite all her training, and the instinctive knowledge that kneeing him in the groin, while not exactly ladylike, would undoubtedly have proved highly effective, she'd done nothing of the sort.

Giving a low moan of shame and mortification, Antonia slumped weakly back against the soft cushions of the large sofa. Staring blindly up at the ceiling, she desperately tried to make some sort of sense of that appalling, hideously embarrassing episode in Lorenzo's suite, only a few hours ago.

How *could* she have become so totally lost to all sense of time and place? How *could* she have allowed herself to be so easily seduced? Not to mention the shame of being caught completely off guard, and at the mercy of her own dangerous, swirling vortex of emotions…?

However, even while freely admitting her own crass stupidity, she wasn't prepared to excuse Lorenzo from blame. Even if he had been provoked, she had no idea what had impelled him to take his revenge by kissing her. It seemed such a strange, bizarre decision that she couldn't seem to make any sense of it.

But she couldn't spare any time sorting out *his* psychological problems. Not when there was still her own problem hanging over her head like the sword of Damocles.

What in the heck was she going to do now?

Unfortunately, never having allowed herself to be involved in this sort of disastrous situation before, she wasn't sure how best to resolve it. Although maybe her ultimatum, issued to Lorenzo in the heat of the moment, had been the right decision, after all? Because until they sorted matters out between them there was no way she and Lorenzo could possibly co-exist in such a close, personal relationship as bodyguard and client.

All in all, it didn't look as if she had any alternative but to immediately resign from the job. Which, to be honest, could only be a great relief. So, perhaps her best course of action would be to inform James Riley, first thing in the morning, that she was no longer prepared to carry out the assignment.

It was going to be hugely embarrassing, of course. Particularly as Lorenzo Foscari was obviously going to make as much trouble for her as he could, with both his insurance company and the Wordwide agency.

You'll just have to tough it out, she told herself with a heavy sigh. There wasn't anything she could do about that. As she'd already decided not to take on any more jobs as a bodyguard, any gossip or scandal wasn't likely to affect the various training courses she was running through her own private security firm.

She had to regard this assignment as just an unfortunate blip, Antonia told herself firmly. Yes, there was no doubt that she'd behaved like a idiot and badly mishandled the whole situation. But it was now time to draw a line firmly under the whole, unfortunate episode—and look forward to a brighter future.

However, as she rose to her feet and walked slowly back through the large sitting room into her bedroom, she had a nasty feeling that extricating herself from all contact with Lorenzo Foscari wasn't going to be quite as easy and trouble free as she hoped.

As it turned out, Antonia's forecast proved to be both right—and wrong.

James Riley was, of course, totally unhelpful and unsympathetic when she contacted him early the next morning. 'You can't do this to me, Tony!' he groaned down the phone.

'I'm really sorry…'

'You must know that it's the busiest time of the year for the agency,' he grumbled. 'There's the tennis at Wimbledon, horse racing at Ascot, the Henley Regatta… you name it, we've got clients flying into London from all quarters of the globe. And they *all* expect a first-class service from us.'

'Yes, I know, but…'

'There's no way I'm prepared to let you off the hook,' he continued grimly. 'We signed a contract, right? And if you even think of trying to wriggle out of it I'll make certain that your name is mud in this business. Got the picture?'

'Don't try and blackmail me, James,' she retorted angrily. 'This isn't just a case of me being petty, or difficult. In fact, and to be entirely blunt, it was a really stupid decision on *your* part to give this guy a female bodyguard. Believe me, he went completely bananas the first moment he set eyes on me! And, after our final confrontation last night, I can virtually guarantee that he's going to insist on me being taken off the case.'

'Oh, yeah...what *did* happen last night?'

'That's none of your business!' she snapped, only too well aware of James's long nose twitching at the thought of a delicious bit of gossip with which to regale their mutual colleagues. 'You can just take it from me that Signor Foscari will be every bit as anxious as I am to terminate my appointment.'

James Riley's heavy sigh of defeat was clearly audible down the line. 'OK, Tony. I'll get on to the insurance company and see what I can work out. I'll get back to you as soon as possible.'

Still feeling the effects of her sleepless night, Antonia munched a piece of toast as she paced angrily up and down the sitting room.

Unfortunately, as much as she would have liked to, there was no way she could just abandon her job. Until James came up with arrangements for her replacement, there was absolutely nothing she could do. In fact, having checked with her minders outside in the corridor that her client was currently enjoying a large English breakfast in his room, she had no choice but to posse herself in patience and wait for her release from an intolerable situation.

When James did ring her back, half an hour later, she was absolutely dumbfounded to hear that Lorenzo Foscari—far from demanding her instant dismissal—had apparently stated that he was perfectly content to retain her services as his bodyguard.

'*What?* What on earth do you mean by "content"?' she demanded incredulously.

'I don't know any more about this business than you do,' James told her flatly. 'I merely rang the insurance company and informed them of the situation. They contacted their client, and have just got back to me with his answer. So, as far as I'm concerned, my agency and the insurance company are fulfilling the terms of the contract—and it's now up to you to do the same.'

'But I can't! I mean, the guy's absolutely impossible to deal with,' she wailed. 'And why the foul man wants to continue this stupid charade...'

'I don't want to know about your problems, Tony—I've got plenty of my own!' James's voice cut ruthlessly across her protest. 'You've got a job to do. So get on and do it!' he added, before putting down the phone.

'Oh, *great*!' she ground out, staring furiously down at the phone in her hand, before slamming it back down. It was all right for James to wash his hands of the whole affair. But what was she going to do now?

After agitatedly pacing up and down the room a few times, Antonia realised that she was just going to have to bite the bullet.

Totally mystified as to why Lorenzo Foscari was, apparently, still prepared to accept her as his bodyguard, she nevertheless had every intention of laying down some hard, fast ground rules concerning their future relationship. Because if that awful man thought that she was prepared to put up with any more of his nonsense he definitely had another think coming!

Fully expecting to have to cope with the arrogant, sardonic character of last night, Antonia was surprised to be greeted by a cool nod of welcome as she marched determinedly into Lorenzo's suite a few moments later.

'Good morning, Miss Simpson,' he drawled smoothly, putting down his newspaper and regarding her with an inscrutable, bland expression from his seat at the small breakfast table.

'It's about time that you and I had a good long talk,' she announced firmly, having already decided that the sooner she took firm control of the situation the better.

'*Sì, d'accordo,*' he murmured, calmly pouring himself a

cup of coffee. 'Yes, I agree. It is clearly time we talked frankly to one another. Have you had breakfast?'

'Yes, thank you,' she muttered, walking over to the window and staring blindly out at Hyde Park Corner as she quickly marshalled her thoughts. This might be the only opportunity she had of setting the record straight. So, she was quite determined to make it crystal-clear that she wasn't prepared to put up with any more of his nonsense.

'Now listen up, Signor Foscari!' she said firmly, turning around to face Lorenzo. 'I don't know what game you think you're playing, or why, for that matter, you've told your insurance company that you're ''content'' to continue with me as your bodyguard. But there's going to be no more nonsense from you, like that which occurred last night. Right?'

Lorenzo put down his cup of coffee, leaning back in his chair, allowing a long silence to develop as he gazed with a bland, enigmatic expression at the girl standing across the room.

'I am quite prepared to ''listen up'', as you put it,' he said at last. 'However, maybe we should first clear the air. No? Because I now wish to tender my complete, unreserved apology concerning that…er…unfortunate incident.'

'You do?' Antonia blinked at him warily.

'There is, of course, no excuse for anyone losing their temper,' he stated firmly. 'I can only imagine that my lapse of good manners was due to a more than usually exhausting business itinerary, and possibly the fact that I was tired after a long day's travel.' He waved a hand dismissively in the air. 'My behaviour was, of course, highly regrettable. However, I can assure you that it will never happen again.'

'You're damn right it won't!' Antonia snapped, slightly thrown by the fact that he appeared to be taking full responsibility for what had happened.

She'd fully expected a difficult if not highly acrimonious interview with this man, and had indeed braced herself to face it. But, now that he'd freely admitted having been well out of order, she wasn't quite sure where to go from here. Buried in thought, Antonia was not aware of the blue eyes glinting with amusement as he viewed the girl standing stiffly by the window.

'May I suggest that we both do our best to forget the whole unfortunate affair?' he murmured soothingly. 'Especially, as I am quite prepared to give you my word of honour that such an incident will never occur again.'

'Well...' She eyed him warily.

'And may I further suggest that you come and sit down—and join me for a civilised cup of coffee? It is rather difficult to try and hold a conversation with someone who is standing on the other side of the room,' he added, accompanying his words with a warm, friendly smile.

Smooth charmer! Antonia told herself, grimly acknowledging the skill and dexterity with which he'd managed to so airily dismiss his rotten behaviour.

Having been determined to be fully in charge of this interview, she now had a disturbing feeling that she was, in fact, dancing to this man's tune.

Unfortunately, she couldn't *quite* put her finger on what was wrong. All the same...Antonia had the distinct feeling that she'd be well advised to keep her wits about her in any future dealings with Lorenzo Foscari.

However, there was clearly nothing to be gained by standing stiffly over here by the window, like a stag at bay. Nor, to be honest, did she wish to have any further discussion about that disturbing kiss last night. Particularly since she was still thoroughly mystified and very cross about her *own* behaviour—let alone his! So, if he was intent on casually dismissing the incident as one of no real importance, it might be a sensible move to follow his example.

'How do you like your coffee, Miss Simpson?' he asked as she moved slowly over the carpet towards him.

'With milk and no sugar,' she said, pulling out a chair and sitting down at the small table.

As he lifted the jug, Antonia studied the man in front of her.

There was clearly no justice in this world! Because, while she'd spent a virtually sleepless night—and was now feeling distinctly the worse for wear—Lorenzo looked as if he'd had an uninterrupted eight hours of refreshing, blameless sleep.

Unfortunately, something strange seemed to have happened to her last night. In the past she'd guarded some famous and *very* handsome men, but Antonia had never had a problem ignoring their manifold attractions and concentrating on her job.

Gazing at Lorenzo's formal white shirt and blue tie, she was suddenly startlingly aware of the way the thin, silky material was clinging so tightly to his muscular torso, emphasising the broad shoulders and slim waist of an extremely fit man.

As he put down the coffee pot and began folding up the newspaper, she found herself staring, mesmerised, at the slim gold watch encircling one of his strong wrists, and at the long, tanned fingers of his hands. Hands which had, only some hours ago, been moving enticingly over her body, and...

For heaven's sake—you've got to get a grip on the situation! she shouted silently at herself, hurriedly raising her cup of coffee to her lips.

'Well, now...' Lorenzo murmured, leaning back in his chair and regarding Antonia from beneath his heavy lids, noting her flushed cheeks and her obvious determination to avoid catching his eye as she stared blindly down at the tablecloth.

Quite what it was that he found so intriguing about this young, highly aggressive woman, he had no idea.

Apart from those startlingly large, clear grey eyes, and an occasional glimpse of an enchanting smile, she certainly wasn't a classical beauty. And, while he was now well aware of the attractions of her slender body—particularly her narrow waist and those warm, deliciously firm breasts—she was obviously not interested in drawing attention to her tall, slim figure.

Clothed in a very severe if undoubtedly smart navy blue suit over a crisp white shirt, she was wearing the minimum of make-up, with her shoulder-length blonde hair brushed into a neat, shining bob, and curling under what could only be called a most determined chin.

Moreover, Antonia Simpson had clearly never found it necessary to use basic, feminine wiles to achieve her ends. He was rapidly coming to realise that this was definitely a lady who possessed attitude with a capital 'A'!

And it was that last point which he found surprisingly refreshing.

Unfortunately, he hadn't been in the best of moods last night, and thus hardly likely to appreciate her extremely efficient way of handling problems—such as the traffic hold-up on the road leading to the Albert Hall.

Of course, that was before he'd had the pleasure of holding her in his arms. And what a revelation that had been! But, leaving that aside, he was now beginning to think that there was a lot to be said for her 'Let's have everything up front' approach to life. At least everyone knew *exactly* where they stood! And it certainly made a pleasant change, he told himself ruefully, from the emotionally exhausting problems currently disturbing his private life, in Milan.

'Well?'

'Hmm?' he murmured, before realising that she was waiting for him to speak. 'Ah, yes. I wanted to tell you that I received a phone call from Italy late last night. The purpose of the call was to inform me that, acting on a tip-off, the police in Rome were closing in on the man who has been issuing threats against my life.'

'You mean...?'

He nodded. 'It looks as if it is merely a question of time before he is apprehended. And, since it now seems highly unlikely that Giovanni Parini will suddenly appear here in Britain, my insurance company has agreed to step down the level of protection.' He shrugged. 'Apparently, I am now in the low risk category, merely requiring a single bodyguard and driver.'

'Well, I imagine you must find that a great relief,' she told him, wondering why she wasn't feeling more elated at being let off the hook. 'I'm sure Worldwide Security will have no problem in providing you with a fully competent man, and—'

'No, you don't understand,' he interrupted sharply. 'I was explaining why I informed the insurers that I was prepared to continue with your services.'

She frowned.

'Quite frankly, Antonia,' he told her with a grin, 'I really don't think I can face *any* more disruption in my life. We may have had a rocky start but at least we do, I hope, now understand one another. And the thought of having to accustom myself to living cheek by jowl with yet another stranger is more than I'm prepared to contemplate.'

'Well...'

'So—do we have a deal?'

She shrugged. 'Yes, I suppose we do,' she answered slowly. 'I'll stand down the other guys, and make arrangements for a professional driver and limo to be on call at all times.'

'Excellent!' He smiled across the table at her.

'I'll need to have a full itinerary of your likely movements for the next few days, of course. And I don't want to have to put up with any nonsense. Such as trying to sneak out of the hotel behind my back,' she added grimly. 'If you want to go to a nightclub, or entertain a woman in your room, I'll make sure I'm fairly invisible, and that you're not disturbed. But you *must* let me know what you're doing. OK?'

'Really, Antonia!' he drawled coldly. 'I'm hardly the sort of man who's likely to behave like that.'

'Oh, yeah?' She gave a caustic laugh. 'We'll see! Believe me, I'm no longer shocked or surprised by some of the antics which even the most staid pillars of society can get up to. Some of the things I've seen would make your hair curl!'

Lorenzo leaned back in his chair, his dark brows creased in a frown as he studied the girl seated across the table. It was clear that this young, attractive woman was used to dealing with the very rough, sordidly unpleasant side of life. A fact which, for some strange reason, he found particularly distressing.

'I think it might be a good idea for you now to tell me something about yourself,' he said at last. 'You must admit that this is an unusual situation,' he added with a slight smile as she quickly raised her eyes towards him. 'What may seem entirely normal to you, in the course of your job, seems, for the ordinary members of the public like myself, a very strange way to earn your living.'

'Yes, well…I suppose you have a point,' she muttered, before once again having the wind taken out of her sails as he announced that he already had full details of her past experience, training with the SAS, et cetera.

How the heck did he find out all that, in such a short space of time? Antonia asked herself grimly. Lorenzo must have moved like greased lightning to have dug out that sort of background information. Which was just one more reason why she'd be well advised to keep a wary eye on this man, who was clearly a very slippery character.

Determined now to play her cards close to her chest, Antonia merely commented, 'It sounds as though you've been rather busy this morning.'

He shrugged. 'I am, of course, regularly in touch with my office in Milan. So it was a very simple matter to ask my secretary to produce the information I required.'

'Hmm...' Antonia murmured sceptically, well aware that since it was now only nine o'clock in the morning this man's poor secretary must have been ousted from her bed at an unearthly hour. Digging out that sort of high-security information would have undoubtedly taken some considerable time.

'OK,' she said, putting down her cup and leaning back in her chair. 'What exactly do you want to know?'

'Well...I do find myself wondering why a very attractive woman would want to spend her days looking after rather dull businessmen such as myself,' he drawled coolly. 'In many ways, I would have thought it a very boring job.'

'Some clients are more dull and boring than others,' she retorted dryly.

'*Touché!*' he laughed, not bothering to pretend that he hadn't recognised her acid comment on his behaviour last night. 'But I understand that you do not solely work as a bodyguard. Correct?'

'Quite correct,' she agreed, before explaining that she now had her own private security firm, the development of which was taking up an increasing amount of time.

He nodded. 'Yes, I can see that might be a good business move on your part,' he commented, before lapsing into silence for a moment. 'However, it occurs to me that, as a woman, you must surely be in demand by Middle Eastern clients, wishing to protect their wives and daughters?'

'Yes, I've done quite a lot of that sort of work in the past. However, I've now decided that I'm not temperamentally suited to jobs of that nature.'

'But surely it must be a constant and rather easy source of income?'

She shrugged. 'Yes, it's lucrative. But, quite honestly, I can't stand all that shopping.' When he lifted a dark, quizzical eyebrow, she added, 'Close-protection work with

Middle Eastern ladies mainly consists of visiting the shops in Knightsbridge or Bond Street.'

'That doesn't sound so bad,' he grinned.

Antonia shook her head. 'No, believe me—you're wrong. It's an absolute *nightmare*! There you are, travelling with an entourage of anything from half a dozen people to a busload of friends, nannies, and often hordes of children as well.'

'Good heavens!'

'Oh, that's not all,' she grinned. 'There are also the servants, who have to be watched like a hawk. They are taken along to order food in restaurants, hold the shopping bags and, *most* important of all, to look after their mistress's designer handbag, which will be crammed with thousands of pounds' worth of fifty-pound notes. And it's the money in the handbag which is the real headache,' she added with a heavy sigh.

He frowned. 'I don't quite see...'

'Unfortunately, it isn't just a matter of guarding the life of the senior Arab wife,' she explained. 'It's also absolutely crucial, that I quickly work out which servant is going to be holding the money. Because every criminal in London is only too well aware that a large, noisy crowd of Middle Eastern ladies will be carrying *huge* amounts of cash. And, for a well organised gang of thieves, they present an unbelievably easy target.'

'Ah!' He gave her a warm, infectious smile. 'So it seems that shopping is now off the menu.'

She nodded. 'As I told one of my colleagues just the other day, I'd be quite happy if I never set eyes on Bond Street ever again.'

As he gave a bellow of laughter and she found herself grinning in response, it was a moment or two before Antonia quickly pulled herself together.

For one thing, she really shouldn't be discussing such matters with a client. And for another...well, there was no doubt that she was instinctively relaxing beneath his warm, charming smile. Unfortunately, Lorenzo Foscari was far too attractive for his own good—and hers!

'Well, Miss Simpson...or may I call you Antonia? Because I think we have gone beyond such formal civilities, don't you? So I suggest that, in private, we call each other by our Christian names.'

She gave him a reluctant nod. 'OK, I'll go along with that.'

'Good. Now, I am sorry to have to tell you, Antonia, that I am about to spoil your day. Because I am intending to visit Bond Street, in order to buy my niece a small present. Possibly a nice string of pearls? Maybe...' He gave her another warm smile. 'Maybe you'd be kind enough to give me some advice?'

Taking a deep breath, and doing her very best to ignore the insidious, subtly beguiling warmth of his smile, Antonia enquired as to the exact age of his niece. When he told her that the girl was only just sixteen, and spending the summer in Cambridge at a language school to improve her English, Antonia quickly shook her head.

'If you'll forgive me for saying so, I think your niece would consider "a nice string of pearls" rather boring. Far too middle-aged. I mean, it's the sort of thing she would expect her mother to be wearing,' Antonia explained as he gazed at her with a slightly puzzled frown.

'At her age,' Antonia continued, 'I'd have appreciated something not so expensive, and far more cool. Maybe an up-to-date watch from Cartier? Or, perhaps, a modern piece of jewellery from Tiffany's might be a better choice?'

'I can see, my dear Antonia, that you are going to prove an invaluable asset during my stay in this country!' he laughed, rising to his feet. 'Therefore, if you can bring yourself to face Bond Street yet again, let us go shopping!'

CHAPTER FOUR

LEAVING the crowded suburbs of London well behind them, and with the A10 motorway opening up before her, Antonia put her foot down hard on the accelerator.

It was the sort of early, bright sunny morning when the English countryside was looking its best. Still damp and sparkling with dew, the patchwork quilt of green fields of wheat and barley, interspersed with woodland and meadows, lay spread out on either side of the road, beneath a brilliant blue sky.

Antonia suddenly felt a rush of pleasure at the prospect of leaving the hot, crowded streets of London. It was many years since she'd visited the ancient university city of Cambridge. And they were obviously going to have perfect weather for the trip.

Glancing briefly at the man sitting beside her, who appeared to be studying the passing countryside with some interest, she found it almost impossible to suppress a broad grin.

Only a few days ago, she'd have been prepared to bet a large sum of money on the fact that Lorenzo Foscari, that oh, so macho Italian, would have preferred to slit his throat rather than allow himself to be driven anywhere by a mere woman!

However, she'd been astounded when, after following his instructions to hire a comfortable sports car—'There's no point in attempting to drive through those narrow English roads in a huge great limousine!'—he'd casually tossed the keys to her, earlier this morning, before lowering himself into the passenger seat of the top-of-the-range Porsche.

'Good Lord!' She grinned at him. 'This is a turn up for the books, isn't it?'

He raised a dark eyebrow. 'I see no reason why you should be so surprised,' he murmured, casting an approving glance at his bodyguard's cream linen trousers and matching jacket, over a pale sage-green silk shirt.

'Well...' She struggled to keep her face straight. 'If you'll forgive me for saying so, Lorenzo, you don't exactly strike me as a man who'd be prepared to accept a *female* chauffeur!'

He gave a brief snort of laughter. 'You are quite right—I'm not. In fact, I can assure you that this is the first time, in my whole life, when I have permitted a woman to tell me what I can and cannot do.'

'Good heavens!' she murmured, rolling her eyes up in mock astonishment.

'So, I decided—as you English would put it—to "go with the flow",' he continued, ignoring her sarcastic interjection. 'Which is why I am now allowing you to drive me around, as well.'

'Oh, wow!' She gave a snort of wry amusement. 'Lucky me!'

'While I may be prepared to accept you as my temporary chauffeur, my dear Antonia, that does *not* mean that I welcome your weird sense of humour,' he informed her sternly as she took her place behind the wheel.

'I'm still not happy about dispensing with the guy who's been driving us around over the past few days,' she told him with a frown. 'Yes...yes, I know—the basic situation has now altered. All the same, I'd prefer to have a back-up—just in case of any trouble.'

'Please stop worrying,' he said, settling himself more comfortably in his seat, and unfolding a map. 'Frankly, I am becoming sick and tired of being smothered in cotton wool. So, if *I* am prepared to take what appears to be a negligible risk, I would appreciate it if *you* would kindly get on with your job.'

'OK…OK, keep your hair on,' she muttered under her breath, taking time to familiarise herself with the controls of the car.

'Well…? What are we waiting for?' he demanded impatiently. '*Andiamo*—Antonia! *Subito…subito.*'

And that was just typical of the man, Antonia told herself now as the car snaked up the road towards Cambridge.

'*Andiamo!*' and '*Subito!*' seemed to be Lorenzo's favourite words. She couldn't recall ever having to put up with a client who demanded service at such a fast pace, she told herself with a grimace. 'Go—go!' and 'At once—at once!' were the words most constantly on his lips. In fact, she seemed to have spent the last few days running as fast as she could, just to keep up with both his demands and his hectic timetable.

There had been one or two lulls, of course. The shopping trip to the dreaded Bond Street hadn't, after all, been quite the ordeal she'd imagined it would be.

Goodness knows what it was about Lorenzo, but whenever they entered a shop it seemed only moments before he was surrounded by a crowd of assistants, all eager and willing to do his bidding.

It must be something to do with that extraordinary charm of his, she told herself sourly. She knew just how difficult and demanding the man could be. And yet she was still apt to find herself weakly succumbing to the full force of one of his long, slow smiles. So it was no wonder that the poor shop assistants had fallen willing, helpless victims to his charm.

And it was the same wherever they went. Even when accompanying him to the offices of a large, prestigious City bank, she'd been astonished at how easily, and with such little effort, he'd managed to charm the socks off the hard-boiled, hatchet-faced woman at the reception desk.

Maybe that's his problem? she mused. Maybe the fairy godmothers at his christening had endowed him with so much personal attraction that he'd always swanned smoothly through life, with virtually every woman he encountered anxious to do all she could to assist him.

On the other hand, Antonia told herself, she wasn't being entirely fair. Lorenzo's male friends and acquaintances, from Giles Harding to the managing director of the large merchant bank, seemed equally happy to be in his company.

In fact, the only person with whom he'd definitely been *less* than charming—initially, at least—had been herself. Although last night, after telling her to book a table for dinner, 'anywhere, just as long as it's reasonably quiet,' she'd definitely felt the full force of his attraction.

Gazing around at the pale walls and sparkling mirrors of the Mirabelle, Lorenzo had flashed her a quick smile. 'It looks as though you have chosen well, my dear Antonia. I can only hope that the standard of cooking will match the decor.'

'It will,' she'd told him confidently, privately keeping her fingers crossed beneath the napkin on her lap because, let's face it, this extremely demanding man had proved to be *very* difficult when having lunch, the day before, in a well-known Italian restaurant.

After sending back one dish, which he'd insisted had not been cooked properly, and complaining when presented with both a chipped plate—'This should not be allowed' and his choice of risotto Milanese—'Disgusting—an utter *travesty* of a great national dish!'—he'd demanded to speak to the manager.

Listening to Lorenzo speaking rapidly in Italian, and obviously telling the man *exactly* what he thought of the food and service, Antonia had noticed the other diners putting down their knives and forks, staring with startled eyes and open-mouthed astonishment at the noisy row being conducted in their midst.

With both men waving their arms, and shouting at the top of their voices in a stream of voluble Italian, Antonia had feared the worst—bracing herself to intervene, and seriously fearing that the argument would descend to actual violence, any moment.

But then—to her complete astonishment—they had suddenly begun laughing, warmly clasping each other's hands and swearing what appeared to be eternal friendship.

Not that he'd been wrong to complain, of course, Antonia had told herself quickly. In fact, if the British spent less time grumbling in private, and complained out loud about bad food and bad service, the standard of cuisine in this country would be a lot higher.

'What was all that about?' she murmured, when a stream of fresh, delicious food had emerged from the restaurant kitchen, and they'd quietly resumed their meal.

Lorenzo gave a casual shrug of his broad shoulders. 'I was just taking him to task about the general level of service. And regretting that the English should think, quite mistakenly, that this was the sort of meal we are accustomed to eating in Italy. A country where we take such matters very seriously, of course.'

'Of course,' she murmured, careful to avoid catching the eyes of the other customers in the restaurant, who were clearly taking some time to recover from having witnessed such a dramatic scene.

He gave another shrug. 'We discovered that both our families come from the same area in Tuscany.'

'I thought you lived in Milan?'

'Yes, so I do,' he agreed. 'But my mother—who is English, by the way—still spends every summer at the old family house in Vallombrosa, in the Pratomagno hills, about twenty miles south-east of Florence, where she looks forward to visits from her children and grandchildren.'

'Is the fact that your mother is English the main reason why you've got such a good command of the English language?' she queried, taking the opportunity to ask a question which had been puzzling her ever since taking on this assignment.

'Yes and no,' he grinned. 'Yes, we did occasionally speak English at home. But I could hardly make myself understood when I was sent over here to go to boarding-school, at the age of thirteen.'

'That seems a bit young to leave home, doesn't it?'

'Possibly,' he conceded. 'But my English grandparents took great care of me, and I used to spend a lot of time at their home in the country, as well as going home to Italy for the holidays. Besides,' he grinned, 'I soon made many good friends at school, with whom I'm still in touch. Like Giles Harding, for instance.'

Unlike lunch, dinner last night at the Mirabelle had been an all-round success. He'd pronounced himself delighted with the food and wine, although she'd had to take his word on the quality of the latter, of course, since she never drank alcohol when on duty.

In fact, the friendly atmosphere had been entirely due to Lorenzo's clear intention of making it a pleasant evening. And, when that determined man set his mind to anything, she was beginning to realise that he very seldom failed to achieve his ends.

Goodness knows how he'd managed it, but somewhere between the succulent lobster and the mouth-wateringly delicious passion fruit *crème brûlé* she'd found herself being soothed and charmed into total relaxation. She'd also, alas, been disgracefully indiscreet about the involvement of colleagues in her own profession in bringing several international criminals to justice.

'I can understand that it is part of your job to be prepared to go anywhere in the world, at a moment's notice,' he commented at one point in the conversation. 'But I must say that I find it quite extraordinary that, in order to protect your client, you see nothing strange in being prepared to risk your life—for a virtual stranger!'

Antonia shrugged. 'Every good, highly professional bodyguard I've known would put themselves in the line of fire, if they had to. It's just something that develops with the training. After all—that's my job. To protect the client. And if that means taking a bullet for them...well, I guess that would just be an instinctive reaction to a dangerous situation.'

'*Dio...Dio...!*' he murmured, staring fixedly at her for a moment, before shaking his head in disbelief. 'What a life!'

'Relax!' she laughed. 'That sort of scenario is *very* rare. And besides, if I allowed myself to feel scared, I wouldn't be able to do my job. I mean...' She hesitated for a moment. 'OK. I'll admit that I've had a few close shaves in the past. But you don't think about it until it's all over. And in any case,' she added, 'I'm generally so aware of everything going on around me that it's rare to find myself involved in something I can't handle.'

However, it was obvious that he found the basic facts of her profession very disturbing, and so she tried to change the subject. But Lorenzo seemed determined to obtain as much information as possible.

'I could not fail to notice, my dear Antonia,' he drawled, 'that your delightful silvery grey silk dress not only cleverly echoes the lovely colour of your eyes, but is also clinging like a limpet to your really superb figure. In fact,' he grinned, 'I have been wondering for the past few minutes exactly *where* you can have hidden your revolver? Or do you carry a gun in your handbag?'

'No, of course not!' she snapped, bitterly aware of the dark flush spreading over her cheeks.

For heaven's sake—pull yourself together! she told herself urgently. It was absolutely ridiculous to find herself blushing at his compliments—and at her age, too!

'Other than for those who serve in the army, or the police force, it is *totally* against the law to carry a firearm here in Britain.

'There are slightly different rules, for guarding members of the diplomatic corps, of course,' she continued. 'And there's no point in pretending that there aren't a considerable number of illegal weapons in circulation. But no *reputable* operative involved in close protection would ever take the chance of breaking that particular law.'

'But surely…surely you must need to learn how to handle a gun? And what happens when you go abroad?'

She shrugged. 'That's a quite different matter. For those of us living in Europe, most of the small arms and automatic weapon training takes place in Cyprus and Turkey. And, of course, if I was working in a dangerous area abroad, I'd arrange to hire a suitable weapon from a local source. Getting "tooled up" in America, for instance, is a breeze!' she grinned.

'But the fact remains,' she added seriously, 'that anyone caught carrying an unregistered firearm in this country would find themselves in deep, *deep* trouble.'

'And quite right too,' he agreed as they rose from the table at the end of the meal. 'Maybe, I've been seeing too many of those gangster films—because I've always assumed that people in your profession would be armed to the hilt.'

'Well, to tell you the truth—although some of my colleagues wouldn't necessarily agree with me—I actually happen to think that guns are a lot more trouble than they're worth.'

He glanced at her in surprise as they walked out of the restaurant, where the chauffeur was waiting beside their limousine.

'There are, after all, any number of methods of foiling the actions of a criminal,' she explained. 'And, short of meeting an armed assailant at point-blank range, I'd feel quite confident of being able to defend myself.'

'Oh, really?' he drawled sardonically, his eyes gleaming with unconcealed mockery as he took his seat in the rear of the vehicle.

You and your big mouth! Antonia told herself grimly.

Unfortunately, she didn't have to be a clairvoyant to know that he was recalling the occasion, only two days ago, when she'd found herself in his arms. Definitely one time when she clearly *hadn't* made a determined effort to defend herself!

As their limousine began moving slowly through the streets of Mayfair, on its way back to the hotel, she could almost feel the atmosphere within the dark, enclosed space at the rear of the vehicle slowly becoming tense and claustrophobic. The bright street lamps were throwing strange, flickering shadows over his austere, hawk-like profile, and she was very conscious of his close proximity.

The occasional touch of his warm, firmly muscled thigh brushing against hers, as their vehicle turned left and right through the narrow maze of streets leading to Park Lane, did nothing for her equilibrium.

Not having had a drop of alcohol, Antonia knew that her rapidly increasing heartbeat and the clammy, damp feeling in the palms of her hands were definitely not drink induced.

Oh, Lord! Don't say that she was making the fatal mistake of falling under this man's spell? No...no, of course she wasn't! The whole idea was completely ridiculous! And, even if he had been subjecting her to a veritable battery of charm this evening, there was no reason on earth why she should become yet another victim of Lorenzo's dangerous, deadly attraction.

Lorenzo was unusually taciturn and uncommunicative as she led him through the front portico of the hotel. 'I believe in always varying one's routine,' she told him. 'There seems no point in giving an opponent an easy ride.'

But he didn't make any comment, nor did he utter a word as they entered the elevator. In fact, it wasn't until she'd escorted him into his suite, to make sure all was in order before going to her own room, that he broke what had become an almost overwhelmingly oppressive silence.

'Would you care for a drink?' he asked.

'No…no, thank you. I think I'll have an early night,' she muttered, disconcerted to find her way barred by his tall, dark figure, leaning casually against the architrave of the sitting-room doorway.

She couldn't think of anything which she might have said or done to upset him. But it was disturbing to find herself feeling intimidated by this man, who'd so suddenly changed from a pleasant dinner companion into a coolly remote, austere figure. Only the glittering blue eyes, staring down at her so intently, seemed to be carrying some sort of obscure message.

Unfortunately, it wasn't one she had time to decipher, as he gave a deep, heavy sigh.

'Forgive me,' he murmured, giving a quick shake of his dark head. Grimacing with self-annoyance, he clasped hold of her hand, before swiftly lifting it to his lips in what was obviously a polite, Continental gesture. 'I have been behaving like a grouch. No?'

'Well…' She shrugged. What could she say? Because he *had* been acting in a thoroughly odd, grumpy manner.

Still, just as long as it hadn't been caused by any action on her part, she had no need to worry. After all, he was the client. So, if he chose to be cantankerous or bad-tempered, that was his business.

All the same…she had the distinct feeling that the sooner she extricated herself from what could be a potentially tricky situation the better. The fact that he was still staring intently down at her, while maintaining his firm grip on her hand, wasn't exactly an ideal scenario, either.

Turning slightly, she gave a very slight tug of her arm, intending it to appear as nothing more than a perfectly normal, casual indication that it was about time she made a move towards her own room.

But, from the brief flicker of wry amusement in his eyes and the almost imperceptible movement of his lips, twitching in silent humour, it was clearly evident that he had no intention of letting her go so easily.

'I must tell you…' He paused, as if searching for the right words. 'The fact is that not only have I enjoyed your company over the past few days, but I now find myself placed in a distinctly awkward position.'

Oh—so that's it! He's decided to give me the sack, she told herself quickly, realising that he might find it difficult, after their very pleasant evening together, to actually put his decision into action.

'It's all right,' she shrugged. Determined to ignore her immediate, instinctive reaction to his decision, which appeared to consist of a strange mixture of disappointment and loss, she gave him a bright, empty smile.

'These things happen,' she added as casually as she could. 'I've thought, right from the beginning, that you really should have been given a male bodyguard. So, if you've decided to dispense with my services, I'll quite understand why…'

'No! You clearly do *not* understand what I am trying to say!' His lips tightened in annoyance for a moment at having to deal with the complexities of the English language.

'On the contrary, my dear Antonia…' he continued softly, raising her hand again and pressing her fingers to his warm lips. 'I wished to make it clear that I now *very* much regret having given you my word of honour the other day.'

Oh, Lord! She'd really got hold of the wrong end of the stick, hadn't she? It looked very much as if—far from wanting to get rid of her services—Lorenzo Foscari now wanted to change the ground rules, to include services of a distinctly personal nature.

Unfortunately, it was no good trying to fool herself any

longer. The aura of dynamic, forceful masculinity, which seemed to positively ooze from every pore of Lorenzo's tall, muscular figure—not to mention that toe-curling, sexy Italian accent of his—was clearly having a disastrous effect on her normally level-headed, down-to-earth personality.

Although, over the last few days, she'd been fiercely determined to deny the fact, Antonia had become increasingly aware that she was teetering on the brink of a dangerous abyss. In fact, if she didn't watch out, she was in serious danger of succumbing to Lorenzo's utterly fatal charm and overwhelming sex appeal...

And—just as clearly—it was obviously now *imperative* that she pull herself together, as quickly as possible.

For almost the first time in her life, she was having to make a determined and strenuous attempt not to give in to an almost overwhelming urge to lean helplessly against that hard, firm body, and feel his strong arms encircling her now trembling figure. But it *had* to be done. And the sooner the better.

'I'm sorry, Lorenzo. I...I meant what I said the other day. This really *is* where I do have to draw the line,' she told him as firmly as she could. 'We've had a very pleasant...er...working relationship. And I'd be sorry if I was forced to tender my resignation.'

For a few moments he stared down at her, his tall figure frozen into sudden stillness. It was impossible for her to read any message in the eyes gazing down at her from beneath their heavy lids. Only a slight tightening of the hand holding her fingers was evidence that this was anything but a pleasant exchange between them.

And yet...somehow it suddenly felt as though she was surrounded by a force-field of crackling electricity, the hair at the back of her neck tingling with alarm and apprehension, and all the nerve-ends in her body quivering with tension.

A few seconds later, she found herself wondering if she'd been mistaken. In fact, it seemed as if the brief episode might have been a product of her over-heated imagination, as Lorenzo gave a nonnchalant, casual shrug of his broad shoulders.

'You are, of course, quite right,' he drawled smoothly. 'I, too, would regret having to accept your resignation. So, please consider my words as having been unsaid, hmm?' he added, quickly pressing his lips to her hand once more, before letting it go.

However, as she made her way to her own room, on legs which felt distinctly unsteady, Antonia caught what she thought was the sound of a heavy sigh as he shut the door of his suite behind her departing figure.

So, maybe he really *had* been making a serious proposition? On the other hand, she told herself firmly, it was far more likely that after a pleasant dinner—and plenty of wine—Lorenzo had merely been exercising his charm a little too freely.

However, if she'd feared that the relationship between them was likely to have been affected by the brief scene in his suite, Antonia soon realised that she'd been quite wrong. In fact, it rapidly became obvious that he'd completely dismissed it from his mind as being a matter of no importance.

Knocking on the door of his suite at the crack of dawn this morning, she'd found that Lorenzo was his normal calm, imperturbable self. Ordering her around like a lackey, as usual, he'd appeared to be in an excellent mood, and clearly looking forward to spending a day in the English countryside.

It had been a deliberate decision on his part to make an early start to the journey, in order to avoid the weekend traffic. But Antonia now found herself having to slow down as she drove carefully through the congested, narrow streets of the centre of Cambridge.

Two of her older brothers had been students here, at Trinity College, and as a young girl she'd frequently visited the town, which contained so many old medieval buildings, some of them dating from the fourteenth century.

Maybe it was a trick of her memory, but the streets now seemed far smaller and more crowded than in the past. So, it was some time before she found herself driving into the underground car park of the hotel, overlooking the green expanse of Parker's Piece, where Lorenzo had arranged to meet his young niece, Maria.

Later, seated in the large comfortable lounge of the hotel, Antonia smiled to herself as she watched the very pretty young Italian girl chatting to her uncle. As she animatedly waving her arms in the air, barely drawing breath as she chatted away in rapid Italian, it sounded as if Maria was ecstatically thanking Lorenzo for his generous gifts.

She was interested to note that, when in the company of a member of his family, he appeared to be far more relaxed and at ease than normal.

He was smiling, even throwing back his head to roar with laughter as Maria related some of her experiences in a strange country. It was clear that not only was he a fond and indulgent uncle, but that his niece held him in no awe whatsoever.

Initially explaining Antonia's presence as being that of merely a friend who'd kindly driven him up from London, Lorenzo had laughingly confessed that it was Antonia who, against his better judgement, had chosen the pair of Paloma Picasso silver earrings with which Maria appeared to be so especially delighted.

During their shopping expedition to Bond Street, and ignoring her freely expressed doubts, Lorenzo had clearly been determined to give his niece a present of real, lasting value. Stubbornly clinging to the idea of 'a nice string of pearls', he'd eventually—after visiting umpteen shops—found what he was looking for at Asprey's.

However, having no problem recalling what she herself would have wanted when Maria's age—despite the possible horror of her elders and betters—Antonia had persuaded him to visit Tiffany's. There, she'd instantly spotted the small, delicate pair of silver earrings, in the shape of an X.

'My sister, Claudia, would definitely *not* regard them as at all suitable,' he'd said dismissively. 'Besides, Maria is far too young to wear such earrings—particularly ones which look as if they are supposed to represent a kiss!' he'd added, frowning with heavy disapproval.

'Hey, relax! There's no need to be so stuffy!' she'd protested. 'They're just a bit of fun, that's all.'

'Claudia has always refused to let her daughter have her ears pierced,' he'd continued, totally ignoring her interjection. 'There is no way she would approve of me giving my niece such a ridiculous present.'

However, after she'd pointed out that the earrings weren't particularly expensive, Lorenzo had allowed himself—much against his better judgement—to be persuaded to add them to his main present.

'You were right—and I was wrong!' Lorenzo now admitted with a rueful grin as Maria leapt to her feet, ignoring the string of lustrous pearls in their silk-lined leather box as she ran across the lounge towards a large mirror on the far wall.

Watching his niece excitedly admiring her reflection— and the small pair of silver earrings nestling in the ears she'd had pierced as soon as she arrived in England—he gave a low rumble of laughter.

'*Dio!* My sister will surely never forgive me! How did you guess?'

Antonia laughed. 'Oh, come on! If you were a young man, leaving home for the first time, and your father had expressly forbidden you to drink any alcohol—what's the first thing you'd do? Quite frankly, Lorenzo,' she added with a grin, 'I'm fairly certain that as soon as possible you'd be in the nearest bar—busy downing a large glass of beer or whisky!'

'Yes, of course. You're quite right, as usual,' he admitted, with another snort of laughter.

'It's no big deal—and she is very young,' Antonia told him with a shrug. 'It's far better for Maria to confine her teenage rebellion to piercing her ears, rather than getting involved with highly unsuitable men.'

'You're so right,' he agreed, rising to his feet as the girl danced happily back across the carpet towards them, impatient to take her uncle and his friend on a tour of some of the old colleges.

'Oh, no—I'm not going in *that*!' Lorenzo exclaimed some time later that morning as he gazed down at the thin, narrow punt, tethered to the bank of the River Cam. 'It looks far too dangerous!'

However hard she tried, Maria was unable to persuade him to join herself and a bunch of young friends on a picnic boating trip up the river to Grantchester, which had apparently been planned for some days.

'You go off and enjoy yourself.' he smiled down at the girl, before giving her a hug and promising to try and see her once again before he left the country.

'Oh, dear—I'm suddenly feeling very old!' Lorenzo murmured with a grin, watching Maria and her friends. Clearly not used to handling a punt, they were struggling to steer the long, narrow boat on what looked like a hazardous, unsteady expedition up river.

'In fact,' he added, after taking Antonia's arm and suggesting that they make their way back to the hotel for lunch, 'I am profoundly thankful that Maria can swim like a fish. Because I have not the slightest doubt that most of those young people will, before long, find themselves in the water!'

Surprised by how pleasant it was to be walking arm in arm with Lorenzo, and how much she was enjoying his company as they strolled slowly up King's Parade, admiring the ancient brickwork of the old colleges, Antonia grad-

ually found her attention being drawn to a possible problem.

The crowds filling the pavement and spilling over on to
the street were far greater than she would have expected,
even for a Saturday morning in late June, when the city
would undoubtedly be crowded with tourists.

If there was one set of circumstances which bodyguards
dreaded, it was those occasions when they found themselves involved in trying to protect their client amidst a
large crowd of people. Not only did it make their job more
difficult, but also far more dangerous. So, while she had no
real expectation of an assassin suddenly emerging from the
mass of people, every instinct told her that she should get
Lorenzo out of this situation as quickly as possible.

Stopping to enquire of some passers-by the reason for
the large crowd, Antonia learned that it was the annual
degree ceremony, held at this time of the year in the Senate
House. An important occasion, usually drawing large
crowds, it was designed for the official bestowal of hon-
orary degrees on distinguished people in public life. It was
also, of course, when degree certificates were given to those
students who had completed their studies, and passed their
final exams that year.

Unfortunately, Lorenzo appeared determined to ignore
her suggestion that they should slip off down a small side
street and avoid being drawn further into the milling throng
of people.

'But no—I find this very interesting,' he said, refusing
to move from where he stood as the crowd parted for the
vice chancellor of the university, in cap and long black
gown trimmed with gold, leading a procession of various
university dignitaries, all of whom were also wearing me-
dieval-style hats and gowns, trimmed with silk or fur.

Definitely uneasy as the noise levels increased, and finding herself jostled by the crowd of people, all craning to
gain a view of the procession, Antonia could only do her
best to stick like glue to Lorenzo's tall figure, constantly

scanning the area around them for any potential trouble-makers.

She was just telling herself that the sooner she extricated her client from this crowd the better, when she was almost deafened by the sound of large explosions.

The air was immediately filled with a cloud of nauseous yellow smoke—and what sounded distinctly like the crack of rapid gunfire.

Without a moment's thought, and acting purely on gut instinct, she swiftly grabbed hold of the back of Lorenzo's jacket, spinning him around behind the shelter of her own figure, while at the same time kicking his legs out from beneath him. Barely a second later, she was crouching protectively over his body, now lying hunched beneath her on the pavement.

Totally ignoring the terrified shouts and screams of the people in the crowd, panic clearly taking hold as they surged helplessly around her, Antonia stared with intense concentration through the drifting cloud of smoke, towards the area from which the gunfire had seemed to originate.

surrounding the area around it are very old—dating from the…'

She was also falling asleep, half on those she enjoyed falling asleep, could guess. She was asleep

CHAPTER FIVE

WHEN thinking about the incident later, it seemed to Lorenzo as if the whole world had suddenly spun violently on its axis, before exploding in a hazy, dense fog of yellow smoke.

There he'd been, quietly minding his own business as he watched the procession making its way to the Senate House—a Palladian style of building, which he'd thought looked interesting—when there had been an enormous Bang… and all Hell had seemed to break loose.

Not that he was able to do anything about it at the time, of course. In fact, he had barely registered the loud noise, before he found himself almost flying through the air, and crashing down hard on the pavement.

Unfortunately, he couldn't remember anything after that. Nothing. A complete blank. And then, as jagged shafts of daylight began to gradually break through the darkness, and it felt as if he was rapidly spiralling upwards through a long, narrow tunnel towards the light, it seemed as though each and every one of his senses was suddenly under assault.

There was an ear-splitting noise of loud shouts and screaming, overlaid with the piercing clamour of what, he slowly realised, must be the sound of police sirens, while the air seemed filled with a strange smell, which he could only liken to that of rotten eggs. He was having difficulty in clearing his bleary vision, which seemed to be confined to a sea of hard grey paving stones—and it felt as though a heavy weight was pressing down on his sore, bruised body.

It wasn't until he was groggily attempting to pull himself together that he became aware of a whole mass of people, milling about in a highly disturbed state of panic. Out of the general mayhem, he heard someone screaming, *'Oh, my God—they're shooting at us!'* and the high-pitched note of terror in the voice produced an even louder volume of wild shrieks, which was almost deafening.

However, his view was restricted to mainly feet and legs, surging around before his dazed eyes. And it wasn't until he found himself being helped up into a kneeling position that he realised it was Antonia, herself, who'd been covering his body.

'Keep calm. There's no need to worry,' she told him, her mouth pressed closely to his ear, in order to make herself heard above the noise. 'It looks as if you might have been knocked out for a while. Do you feel OK?'

It seemed to take a long time before he understood what she was saying.

'*Sì.* Yes. Yes, I...I think so.'

'Can you manage to stand up?'

He nodded his dazed head, grateful for the girl's strength as she helped him to stagger to his feet.

'I shouldn't move you, if you've had concussion. But if this crowd gets any more out of hand you're in serious danger of being trampled underfoot,' she shouted, placing one of his arms over her shoulder. 'We've got to get out of here—as fast as possible!'

Determinedly elbowing her way through the milling horde of people, she steered them along the road, towards a nearby church.

Still trying to focus his hazy vision, Lorenzo felt as if he was somehow moving through a dream landscape, the feeling of total unreality still gripping his dazed mind as they entered the church porch.

'I don't know what's going on,' she said, helping him to sit down on one of the hard stone benches running down each side of the porch. 'But, at least it's a bit quieter in here.'

Brushing the dust from her cream trousers, and pacing up and down over the flagstones, Antonia ran the sequence of events back and forth through her mind, before sitting beside him.

'I'm almost certain that it wasn't real gunfire,' she said slowly. 'And, with any luck, the police will soon have things under control.'

'*Va bene…*' he murmured, leaning back against the ancient stonework and shutting his eyes for a moment as he tried to pull himself together.

'Oh, dear—I don't like the look of that,' he heard her mutter under her breath, and a moment later was aware of her removing the silk handkerchief from the top pocket of his jacket.

'*Che…?*' he murmured. 'What…what is it?'

'You seem to have a slight cut on your head,' she told him as she leaned across the long, tall figure seated beside her, carefully dabbing the graze on his forehead.

Concentrating on her task, and frowning at the bruised, small area of grazed skin which was already swelling up into a hard lump, she glanced down to see that Lorenzo's eyes were now wide open, staring fixedly at her face, only inches away from his own.

Much later, when trying to account for what happened next, Antonia could only conclude that both she and Lorenzo *must* have been in a bad state of shock, due to the explosion. It was the only explanation which seemed to make any sense at all.

Unfortunately, she had no idea that there was anything wrong with her as she found herself gazing deeply into Lorenzo's glittering blue eyes. No prior warning of the fact that, for some odd reason, the noisy clamour in the street was now becoming strangely muted. Nor could she account for why the daylight within the porch appeared to be gradually shrinking about them, until there remained nothing but an oasis of calm silence amidst the dark void surrounding their two, still figures.

It was…it was as if all the clocks had suddenly stopped ticking. The very concept of time, as a measurement of minutes and seconds, appeared to have no meaning as they sat staring at one another. She was only aware of a drowsy, rather peculiar feeling of heavy languor as he slowly raised his hand to take the handkerchief from her fingers.

'You have a mark on your cheek,' he murmured, his quiet voice barely audible as he gently brushed the dusty smudge from her face.

Feeling strangely dizzy and disorientated, she could only gaze helplessly at him as he discarded the thin piece of silk, allowing his fingers to move slowly through the fine strands of blond hair, falling across her cheek, to softly caress the back of her neck.

Seemingly unable to move, and hardly able to breathe, she could feel her heart suddenly beginning to thud, pounding loudly against her breast at the warm, soft touch of his fingers moving gently down her neck. She shivered as his hand slipped inside her linen jacket, sliding over the thin silk shirt to lightly caress her breast. Gasping helplessly at the erotic movement of his thumb, drawing soft circles around her hard, swollen nipple, she couldn't seem to stop trembling, as if suffering from a high fever. She felt his other arm closing slowly about her, drawing her closer to him, until she was aware of his breath softly fanning her face, her nostrils teased by the faint, elusive scent of his cologne.

And then, at the feather-light touch of his warm lips on hers, it was as though her whole world was suddenly bursting into an explosive display of brilliant fireworks—just as if someone had idly tossed a lighted match into a quiet, still pool of gasoline.

A fast running stream of liquid fire was flooding through her veins, her stomach muscles tensing into a hard knot of feverish need and desire as she pressed her lips hungrily to his. And, as she trembled in his arms, it seemed as if he, too, had become possessed by the same mad sexual frenzy, his mouth and tongue becoming more demanding, burning hotly as his arms tightened about her, pressing her firmly to his hard, muscled body. And she…she had no thought but to yield…to melt helplessly against him in total surrender.

Utterly consumed by the devouring force of hunger and passion, Antonia took some moments before she became aware that they were no longer alone.

'Yeah…I reckon she'll be all right in here,' a burly man was saying to his male companion as they peered in through the arched doorway of the church porch.

With a horrified gasp, Antonia tore herself from Lorenzo's arms, her cheeks burning with embarrassment as she quickly leapt to her feet.

'Sorry, folks—but this poor old lady isn't looking too good,' the man said as he and a younger man helped an elderly, frail-looking woman inside the porch.

'Is…is there anything I can do?' Antonia muttered, not daring to glance in Lorenzo's direction as she hurried over to offer her assistance.

'Thanks, love,' the man said as she helped them to settle the woman down on a stone seat on the opposite side of the porch to where she and Lorenzo had been sitting.

'No…you stay where you are,' Antonia said, avoiding looking directly at Lorenzo's tall figure as he, too, rose slowly to his feet. 'I…I'll go and get help,' she added quickly, almost running out of the porch in an effort to escape the scene of her totally incomprehensible, utterly shameful behaviour.

'Fire-crackers?' Lorenzo exclaimed, some considerable time later. 'Are you seriously telling me that it was only fire-crackers and a few loud stink bombs, let off by some

silly students, which are responsible for my being here, in this hospital?'

'Yes, I'm afraid so. Although it's my fault that you received that bump on your head,' Antonia reminded him with an apologetic grimace.

But when he only muttered something unintelligible under his breath she turned back to gaze out of the window of the private room which had been temporarily allocated to Lorenzo.

Despite doing her best to concentrate on looking after her client, she was still having a problem coming to terms with the extraordinary episode which had taken place in the church porch.

This was the first time they'd been left alone with one another since arriving here at the hospital. Which meant that she still hadn't a clue how he was likely to react to the incident. Not that she was in a hurry to find out, she assured herself quickly. Lorenzo might have remained silent on the subject so far, but she couldn't help feeling distinctly nervous, whenever she caught his totally enigmatic, inscrutable gaze turned in her direction.

Anxious to avoid any reference to the highly awkward subject, she said quickly, 'If it's any consolation, you're not the only casualty. At least ten other people have ended up here, suffering from anything from a broken leg to concussion. When panic sets in,' she added, 'a large crowd of people in a confined space can easily escalate into a very dangerous situation.'

'Thank you for the lecture on personal safety,' Lorenzo snapped irritably. 'But I'm far more interested in hearing when they're going to let me out of here.'

'Yes, well, I...er...I'll just go and check with the doctor...' she muttered, quickly seizing the opportunity to leave the room.

How *could* she have behaved in such an unprofessional

manner? Antonia asked herself for the umpteenth time as she hurried down the hospital corridor.

It *must* have been the shock of the explosion, she told herself helplessly. There was simply no other explanation which made any kind of sense. And what on earth she was going to say—if or when Lorenzo referred to the incident—she had absolutely no idea.

On the other hand, there was no doubt that Lorenzo really *had* been stunned and shocked by the explosion. So, there was a good chance that he might not be able to recall the disastrous incident, Antonia comforted herself as she entered one of the huge bank of elevators. But she had a horrid feeling that she was clutching at a broken straw.

As Antonia left the room, Lorenzo gave a heavy sigh, throwing himself back on the pillows, and wondering what he'd ever done to deserve such a fate.

Antonia Simpson might well be good company, and one of the most unusual women he'd ever met. Unfortunately, he had to face the fact that he was finding her far too attractive and distracting for his own good. Besides, he had a full, busy life in Milan—and enough romantic complications there, with Gina Lombardi, without needing to add to his current problems.

Which was why—leaving aside the question of his totally inexplicable behaviour—he had *no* intention of repeating his mistake of earlier today. A decision he'd come to within minutes of Antonia leaving him in the church porch, while she went to get help for both himself and the old lady.

Quite how long it had taken her to gain assistance Lorenzo had no way of telling. But it hadn't seemed long before an ambulance had arrived outside the church, with Antonia clearly in charge of the operation.

'My client—and this old lady too, of course—needs to be taken immediately to hospital,' she'd announced in a firm voice, brandishing an official-looking card in a plastic wallet, which had clearly impressed the ambulancemen, who'd hurried to do her bidding. It was only much later that he realised that it must have been Antonia who'd also been instrumental in making sure that the ambulance took as many of the other wounded to hospital as possible.

However, on arrival at the casualty department, Lorenzo had finally managed to pull himself together, and get a grip on the situation.

Protesting that he was perfectly all right, he'd tried to insist that he had no need of the brain scan which Antonia was so firmly demanding. Unfortunately, it appeared that not only was she responsible for his head wound, which had rendered him momentarily unconscious, but she was quite prepared to cause as much trouble as possible until she got her own way.

He might have been blind, deaf and dumb for all the notice anyone had taken of him, Lorenzo told himself grimly, recalling how Antonia had kept on insisting that her 'client' be checked over from head to toe, until, possibly out of sheer exhaustion, the doctors had caved in and done as she requested. Although, as he could have told them in the first place, there had been nothing at all wrong with him.

But Antonia had been entirely unrepentant. 'Better to be safe than to be sorry,' she'd declared firmly, before grabbing hold of a young doctor and insisting that Lorenzo's wrist, which had been slightly strained during his fall, should be firmly strapped up.

'This is ridiculous!' he'd grumbled angrily. 'I didn't notice it at the time, and I can hardly feel it now. Besides, how can I cope with my right hand bandaged in this way?'

'Very easily, I imagine,' Antonia had murmured sardonically, grinning over his body at the handsome young doctor, before adding, 'Especially since we both know that you're left-handed!'

Now, as he turned sideways to pick up the glass of water from his bedside cabinet, Lorenzo glared down at his right wrist, firmly taped up with some sort of bandage, and held in a sling, close to his chest.

The fact that the doctor had said he'd probably be able to remove the bandage tomorrow was of little consolation, he told himself grimly. And, even though he'd been given the best private accommodation currently available, it didn't help to make his enforced sojourn in this place any more acceptable.

'I'm sorry, but there's nothing I can do to hurry things along,' Antonia said as she returned to the room, some minutes later. 'It seems that the police are insisting on taking a brief statement from you, since they may well be prosecuting the students who let off those explosions.'

'That's all I need!' he grumbled, glaring up at the girl standing beside his bed. 'I hope you realise that this is all your fault!' he grated. 'There's such a thing as being *too* keen on the job, you know,' he added with heavy sarcasm.

'Never mind—we should be out of here fairly soon,' she told him, calmly refusing to rise to the bait. Besides, the man had a point. While the student prank had, of course, been nothing to do with her, there was no doubt that her anxiety to protect him, at all costs, was solely responsible for that nasty bump on his head.

After the visit from a young policeman, which was mercifully brief, the young doctor breezed into the room, clearly interested in furthering his brief acquaintance with Antonia—to whom he'd clearly taken a shine.

'Well, it looks as if you got off fairly lightly,' the man told him in a cheerful, hearty voice. 'That bodyguard of yours is a really terrific girl, isn't she? I wouldn't mind a bit of danger if I could have *her* looking after me!' he added with a raucous laugh.

'But, as it turned out, there *was* no real danger,' Lorenzo pointed out coldly, his instinctive dislike of this brash young man, whom he'd first met in the casualty department, now deepening into outright animosity.

'Well, I suppose you're technically right, but I reckon you ought to be damn grateful to have someone not only prepared to save your life, but also willing—by shielding you with her own body—to keep you safe from any harm.'

Lorenzo realised that there was no point in arguing any further with this truculent young man, who clearly had fallen hook, line and sinker for Antonia.

More fool him! he thought, closing his eyes and leaning wearily back against the pillows as the other man left the room. That young doctor would soon change his tune if he had to spend more than a few days with that highly irritating woman. Even he wasn't likely to appreciate someone constantly telling him what to do—morning, noon and night.

Besides...he didn't need to have some young whippersnapper pointing out the obvious. Because he was perfectly well aware that Antonia was basically a very brave woman. Just as he was equally capable of appreciating the fact that, if he *had* been in any real danger, her actions would undoubtedly have saved his life. For which he would, of course, have been exceedingly grateful.

Nevertheless, the fact remained that he was now lying here in this hospital with a bandaged wrist, his body covered in bruises, and a thumping headache, which was getting worse by the minute. And he did not, at the moment, feel *at all* grateful to the woman who—for some extraordinary reason he couldn't even begin to fathom—appeared to be causing total havoc in his personal, private life.

However, when Antonia returned to his room and, after taking one look at Lorenzo, rang a bell for a nurse and insisted that he should be given something to help cure his headache, he decided that maybe...just maybe...she had a few good points, after all.

'OK. The doctor says that you can go now,' Antonia informed him as he swallowed the aspirins.

'Humph!' Lorenzo grunted, grimacing as he raised himself up against the pillows. He was feeling tired, sore and generally fed up to the back teeth with life in general—and this woman in particular. So, the prospect of a long journey back to London wasn't exactly something he was looking forward to.

'I'm afraid this isn't a brilliant job—but it's the best I could manage, under the circumstances,' Antonia told him, taking his suit out of the wardrobe.

Quite frankly, there hadn't been much she could do about the state of his clothes. However, one of the nurses had been very kind, helping her to brush the dust and dirt from his trousers, and to steam-press the jacket. So, although Lorenzo—who always appeared totally immaculate, at all times—was now eyeing the garments with a distinctly jaundiced eye, he was going to be able to walk out of this hospital looking halfway decent, at least.

She hesitated for a moment before placing the suit on a chair near his bed. 'Would you like either myself or a nurse to help you put on your trousers?'

'Absolutely not!' he snapped. 'I'm perfectly capable of seeing to that sort of thing for myself.'

'OK…fine…' She gave a slight shrug, trying not to smile at the look of horror on Lorenzo's face. Did he really think that she'd never seen a guy's legs before now? 'I'll be just outside, if you need me,' she added, walking towards the door.

Fairly certain that, in this bad mood of his, her client would have to be utterly desperate to seek her assistance, Antonia leaned against the wall in the corridor, prepared for a long wait.

She actually felt very sorry for the poor guy, who'd really been put through the mill today. He was the victim of an extremely unfortunate set of circumstances, and it was no wonder that his temper—clearly slightly unstable at the best of times, if her previous experience with that gentleman was anything to go by!—was now on a shorter fuse than usual.

However, she knew that if she ever again found herself in the same situation she would still take the necessary action to protect her client. It was obvious that Lorenzo was feeling thoroughly fed up with her—something she could well understand. But, although one hardly expected to find villains running amuck in a relatively peaceful town in East Anglia, far more bizarre things had happened in the past.

None of which was likely to be of any comfort to Lorenzo, of course. But at least his anger with life in general—and herself in particular—was preventing any discussion between them regarding that mind-blowing kiss in the church porch, when he...

Oh, no! She was *not* going to think about it—*ever again*! she told herself fiercely, bitterly aware of the flush rising over her cheeks at the fleeting recollection of the soft, warm lips and muscular body, pressed so tightly to her own.

She had just about managed to pull herself together when Lorenzo finally opened the door and emerged out into the corridor.

So she'd been quite right in guessing his determination not to ask for help, Antonia thought, gazing at the man who was looking thoroughly annoyed and exasperated.

Walking slowly down the hospital corridor, she asked him whether he wanted her to inform his niece, Maria, that he'd been involved in the accident.

'It's sure to feature strongly in the local paper,' she pointed out. 'And I suppose it might occur to her that you could have been one of the people who were injured.'

'Definitely not,' he retorted curtly. 'There is absolutely no point in worrying the child. Especially as there is nothing wrong with me. In fact, I will probably telephone her from London tonight and allow her to tell me all about the incident,' he added as they took the lift down to the ground floor of the hospital.

'How on earth did *that* get here?' he demanded, staring with surprise at the black Porsche parked just outside the main doors of the hospital.

Antonia shrugged as she held open the passenger door for him.

'While you were having your brain scan, I decided it might be a good move to collect it from the car park at the hotel. So, hop in.'

'I don't feel like hopping *anywhere*!' he said tersely, before gingerly lowering his bruised body into the low-slung seat. The fact that he had to suffer the further indignity of requiring Antonia to help him with his seat belt did nothing to improve his temper.

Leaning back against the head-rest, Lorenzo closed his eyes and gave a heavy sigh. It was not only pointless, but also unfair to take his general bad temper out on Antonia. She might have been partly responsible for the debacle in which he found himself—but he had to admit that she'd done her best to sort out the mess.

Quite why he'd allowed himself to become so unusually stressed out he had no idea. And he *really* didn't want to think about the extraordinary episode which had taken place between himself and Antonia earlier in the day. Which was proving extremely difficult, when he was acutely aware of sitting so close to her slim figure.

After all, he was only going to have to suffer this woman's attentions for a few more days—if he didn't sack her, the moment he got back to London!—and then he could return to his normal, well-ordered life in Milan.

Although, if he were honest, his life hadn't been particularly restful or tranquil in Milan over the past few months.

Women! They really were the very devil to cope with—however beautiful they might be. And there was no doubt that Gina Lombardi was an outstandingly beautiful-looking woman.

Initially attracted by not only Gina's looks but also her

apparently mild and placid temperament, Lorenzo and she had become an item, with Gina acting as a very gracious hostess whenever he'd felt it necessary to entertain friends in his large apartment in the centre of Milan.

To be truthful, no one could accuse the lovely girl of being an intellectual giant. But, nevertheless, she'd been a highly decorative companion. And so matters had continued, for the past year.

Unfortunately, what Lorenzo had always thought of as his fairly restful, tranquil life now appeared to be in danger of being actively disturbed. His lips tightened as he recalled his own stupid, foolish reluctance to resolve what was becoming a tricky situation.

Having searched his conscience, he was quite clear in his own mind that he had *never*, at any point, allowed Gina to believe that she would have a permanent place in his life. In fact, he'd always been very careful to make sure she clearly understood that there was no question of her moving into his bachelor apartment. Because although he'd enjoyed her company, both in and out of bed, there had never been any question of their relationship ending in marriage.

Despite having had many glamorous girlfriends in the past, he'd never yet met the one woman with whom he wished to share the rest of his life—to be the mother of his children and—a very important point as far as he was concerned—someone of whom his beloved *mamma* would approve.

It might seem strange that, having reached the age of thirty-eight, he still regarded it as important that his mother should have a good opinion of his future wife. But she was, without doubt, one of the cleverest and shrewdest women of his acquaintance. Which was one of the reasons why he'd never taken any of his girlfriends to the family home in Tuscany.

The fact that his mother had clearly disliked Gina, whom she'd met when staying with him in Milan last year, hadn't helped matters, of course. Especially just lately, when a distinct change had suddenly come over his girlfriend, who now seemed almost obsessed with the urge to marry him. Even forcing himself to be unkind, and bluntly pointing out that he wasn't in love with her, had done little to clear up the situation.

Gina was now making constant references to the fact that her 'time-clock' was running out, creating dramatic scenes and weeping all over his carpets. Exactly why she should be so very keen to nail him down he had no idea. But, while he must obviously end the affair as soon as possible, it was equally obvious that he couldn't just dump someone with whom he'd had such a long relationship.

Maybe he ought to buy her a new apartment, as a parting gift? Although, knowing Gina, Lorenzo told himself sardonically, she would undoubtedly prefer a large, highly expensive piece of jewellery, and a flashy car!

Unfortunately, he'd been far too busy lately to spend the time either sorting out or resolving the situation. Something which he must clearly do as soon as possible, on his return to Milan.

Having come to a sensible, rational decision, Lorenzo opened his eyes, and noted with surprise that they were now travelling slowly through a small country village.

That's odd, he told himself with a frown. He was almost sure...no, he was certain that they hadn't taken this route earlier this morning.

'I don't remember this village.' He turned his head to gaze at Antonia. 'Are we returning to London by a different road?'

'No. After the events of today, I didn't think you'd want to face a long journey,' she told him. 'So, I phoned my brother and his wife, and arranged for us to spend the rest of the weekend with them.'

'You did *what*?'

'You're clearly feeling tired and weary. Which is why I reckoned you needed a hot bath and a comfortable bed as

soon as possible,' she added hurriedly, bracing herself for
the strong objections of her passenger, who appeared to be
in a really foul mood.

She was quite right—he was.

In fact, Lorenzo found he was deriving considerable satisfaction from being able—at last!—to give voice to his
long list of complaints. Freely expressing his views on her
suitability as a bodyguard, he then turned his attention to
those aspects of her character which he found *particularly*
annoying. Specifically, her unbelievably arrogant, dictato-
rial and high-handed attitude to men in general—and himself in particular!

Antonia concentrated on her driving, deliberately closing
her ears and ignoring the storm of rage filling the vehicle.

Weary, bruised, and in need of a good night's sleep,
Lorenzo was clearly at the end of his tether. Which was
why she'd had no compunction about deciding to take him
to her brother's house, in a village only a few miles outside
Cambridge.

'Feeling better now?' she asked, slowing down and turning off the road, before turning to give him a wry smile as
he finally ran out of steam.

There was a long, heavy silence as she drove through a
pair of tall iron gates, and on down a long gravelled drive,
before Lorenzo finally gave a snort of harsh, rueful laughter.

'Yes…you utterly horrible woman—I am!' he admitted
with another grim laugh as she finally brought the vehicle
to a halt outside a large mansion. 'But don't push your luck,
hmm?'

'I wouldn't dream of it,' she murmured, which produced
another cynical grunt of laughter as she switched off the
engine, and turned towards the man sitting beside her.
'OK…here we are,' she said. 'Just to put you in the picture:
my brother's name is Tom Simpson, and he's a professor
of medieval history at Cambridge University.

'His wife's name is Flavia,' she continued. 'Not only is
she very nice, but she also happens to be very wealthy in

her own right. Which, since university professors do not earn high salaries, is how they come to be living in a house of this size,' Antonia explained, getting out of the car and coming around to open the door for Lorenzo.

'By the way,' she added, 'I know that you're tired and fed up. But I would be grateful if you could make an effort to be pleasant to them, at least.'

Not deigning to take any notice of such impertinence—how could she possibly imagine that he would be guilty of such crass bad manners?—Lorenzo unwound his tall figure from the small sports car. Stretching his limbs, he gazed up at the building before him.

The setting sun was casting a crimson glow over the tiled roof of the very large old Jacobean manor house which, from its mullioned windows and the big front door, heavily studded with iron bolts, had clearly remained unchanged for the past four hundred years.

With the sound of pigeons cooing in the nearby tall oak trees, and the sight of sheep contentedly nibbling the rich green grass of the parkland surrounding the house, it was a restful, harmonious scene of peace and tranquillity. Lorenzo took a deep breath, feeling himself slowly beginning to relax, at last.

CHAPTER SIX

WITH Antonia leading the way, they were halfway across the gravel forecourt when the large oak front door was wrenched open.

A moment later, a woman was running towards them, with her arms outstretched and speaking so fast that it was a moment or two before Lorenzo could make out what she was saying.

'Oh, my dears! I've never heard anything quite so awful! We've just been watching it all on the local news. Those students! What *will* they think of next?' she cried, barely drawing breath as she quickly embraced Antonia.

'And you must be Lorenzo!' she exclaimed, turning swiftly towards him.

'Yes. This is very kind of you, but...'

'You poor man! Antonia's told us *all* about it. I'm *so* sorry this should have happened on your trip to England—hardly what one wants on a holiday, is it?' she added, slipping a hand through his left arm and looking with concern at his other wrist, still bandaged and held in a sling against his chest.

'My dear—how awful! I *do* hope that you aren't in too much pain?'

'No...not at all. I...'

'And you must be so fed up. I know what hospitals are like,' she continued, happily ignoring anything he might say as she carefully led him through the front door and into the large, spacious hall. 'It's all hard beds and nasty syringes, isn't it? The poor nurses are paid an absolute *pittance*, and run off their feet. The young doctors are totally overworked, and fall asleep all over the place. While the fat-cat consultants hardly look at you before demanding quite *outrageous* fees! And no one has the *faintest* idea of how to make anyone feel really comfortable, have they?'

Just beginning to wonder whether that blow to his head, earlier in the day, had actually left him brain-damaged, Lorenzo caught Antonia's eye.

He was much relieved to note that she was regarding her voluble sister-in-law with a wide grin of fond amusement. So, it looked as if his mind was still in good working order, and that this really *was* his hostess's normal mode of speech.

By the time he found himself seated in a deep, comfortable armchair, sipping a hot cup of tea and being pressed to have yet another slice from the deliciously moist, large chocolate cake, Lorenzo was beginning to think that he might survive the next twenty-four hours, after all.

In fact, he was finding it remarkably relaxing to have this slim, petite and very pretty titian-haired woman sympathising with his recent ordeal, and clearly determined to try and make her guest feel as much at ease as possible.

A sharp contrast to her sister-in-law, he thought, turning a caustic eye in the younger woman's direction. Flavia, who was clearly hanging on his every word, obviously understood the art of soothing a man's ruffled feathers.

Antonia, who had no problem in accurately reading his mind, was deriving some considerable amusement from the situation.

Like every man she'd ever met, Lorenzo was clearly enjoying having a great fuss made of him. But just wait until he'd sampled dinner tonight. Because if he thought that Flavia—who *had* to be the world's worst cook—had made that delicious chocolate cake with her own fair hands he was sadly mistaken!

She dearly loved Flavia—quite the nicest of her three sister-in-laws—but Antonia had no illusions about the older woman. A highly successful artist, specialising in portraits of well-known men and women, Flavia might have convinced Lorenzo that she was hanging on his every word. But Antonia knew that she was barely listening to what her guest was saying.

Those wide green eyes, staring so fixedly up into his face, were far more likely to be noting the planes and angles of his high cheekbones. In fact, Antonia was almost certain that the older woman was, right this minute, considering which mixture of oil paints would best reproduce the various flesh tones of his tanned skin.

Maybe she ought to have warned Lorenzo that Flavia would undoubtedly drag him off to her studio, as soon as possible, unable to resist experimenting with a fresh subject?

But no, Antonia told herself quickly. Even she was prepared to admit that he'd had a really rough day. It would be far better to let the poor man have a good night's sleep before the full glory of Flavia's obsession with her art—*and* her lack of even the most basic housekeeping skills—burst upon him in all their glory!

Temporarily distracted from her urgent desire to draw Lorenzo by the entry into the room of her husband, Flavia quickly introduced Tom to their visitor.

'This poor man has had a simply *dreadful* time,' she said as Antonia jumped up to give her brother a kiss. 'We must make sure that he has a really restful time here in the countryside.

'London is *so* noisy and full of car fumes, I don't know *how* you can bear it!' she added, turning to Lorenzo with a warm, sympathetic smile. 'I do hope you will feel able to stay here with us—for the rest of the weekend, at least.'

Giving her husband a quick nudge—dear Tom was totally immersed, at the moment, in the book he was writing about medieval warfare, and hardly knew what day it was—she was pleased when he, too, urged their guest to make himself at home, for as long as he liked.

'I'd be very pleased to accept your kind invitation,' Lorenzo murmured, clearly not able to face the thought of having to get back into the car for the journey to London. 'There is, however, a slight problem,' he added, and explained that neither he nor Antonia had brought a change of clothing with them.

Luckily, it was Antonia—really such a *clever* girl, Flavia told herself, giving her sister-in-law a beaming smile—who pointed out that, while the two men had quite different physiques, they were both slim and approximately the same height.

'I think he could well fit into some of your jeans, shirts and sweaters,' Antonia pointed out to her brother, before turning to Lorenzo.

'This is practically my second home. So finding myself something to wear isn't a problem. And I don't suppose you feel like being madly social, and meeting any of the local gentry. So, providing that Tom's clothes are a reasonably decent fit, it won't matter too much if you aren't looking your usual smart self, will it?'

Agreeing that, no, it didn't matter a bit, Lorenzo willingly accepted the offer of his host's spare clothing, and his kind invitation to spend the weekend. In any case, he was feeling far too exhausted to contemplate leaving tonight.

Woken the next morning at an unearthly hour, by the sound of a blood-curdling screech just outside his window, Lorenzo leapt out of bed, moving swiftly across the room and throwing open the mullioned casement window. Only to find himself staring down at a large peacock strutting back and forth across the lawn.

Muttering various oaths under his breath, mostly concerning the mad British and their inexplicable fondness for strange animals, he staggered back to bed, falling asleep again almost immediately.

Woken again some hours later by a knock at the door, he opened his eyes to see Antonia entering the room, carrying a tray in her hands.

'I hope you're feeling better today?' she murmured, setting the tray down on a table beside the bed. 'How's that sore wrist of yours?'

'It seems fine,' he said, glancing down at his bandaged limb as he raised himself up against the soft feather pillows, realising that he did indeed feel very much better. 'Although, to be honest,' he added with a grin, 'I could have done without being woken so early this morning by that damned bird!'

'It's a flaming nuisance, isn't it?' Antonia agreed with a sympathetic, if slightly nervous smile.

It was proving difficult to keep her eyes away from the large amount of wonderfully smooth, tanned skin covering Lorenzo's strong arms and broad shoulders—not to mention his wide, muscular chest, liberally sprinkled with black, curly hair.

This man should be stamped with a government health warning, she told herself crossly. So much erotically enticing male flesh was obviously highly dangerous!

'It was a peacock I saw out on the lawn?'

'What? Oh, yes, it was,' she muttered, quickly making an effort to pull herself together. 'Unfortunately, Tom and Flavia were given the peacock as a thank-you present from an American guest,' she added, strolling across the room towards the window. 'Although quite *why* he chose such a bizarre gift no one quite knows.'

'Not my idea of the perfect present for one's hostess,' he agreed with a grin, his gaze travelling over Antonia's trim figure, dressed in a crisp, short-sleeved white linen shirt, tucked into a pair of tight blue jeans.

It was the first time he'd seen her wearing casual clothes, and it occurred to him that she was looking much younger and far more relaxed than when formally attired in a smart London suit.

'Unfortunately Flavia can't persuade anyone else to take on the peacock—and is far too soft-hearted to strangle the beastly bird!' Antonia told him, leaning casually against the window, feeling more relaxed now that she'd put some distance between herself and the man in the bed.

While she'd been speaking, Lorenzo had been cautiously eyeing the contents of the tray. After having been presented at dinner last night with the most *dreadful*, utterly inedible meal he'd *ever* had the misfortune to come across, he had no expectation that breakfast was likely to be any better.

However, as he noted the freshly squeezed orange juice, his nostrils absorbing the delicious aroma of newly made coffee, he decided that maybe he might not starve during the weekend, after all.

'You can relax!' Antonia's eyes gleamed with laughter, once again accurately reading his mind. 'Flavia isn't in the slightest bit interested in food, and never has breakfast herself. So we normally help ourselves. It's generally guaranteed to be the only meal you can get in this house that's worth eating,' she added ruefully.

'Yes…er…that dinner last night was…well…to be totally frank, my dear Antonia, I have to say that I have *never* had such an appalling meal!' Lorenzo confessed with a slight laugh.

She grinned. 'Oh, yes—everyone knows that Flavia's cooking is absolutely atrocious. I think it must be the artistic temperament,' she added reflectively. 'She really does try and do her best, but the poor darling had clearly forgotten to cook the chicken breasts—or to remember that mashed potatoes need mashing…'

'*Please!*' He raised a hand. 'If you don't mind, I'd prefer to try and forget the whole, utterly horrible experience.'

'I don't blame you!'

'Although,' he added dryly, 'I now find myself wondering whether your sister's American guest might not have taken a subtle revenge on his hostess.'

'Revenge?'

'Well, if he had sampled Flavia's version of *raw* chicken suprême, he might have deliberately presented her with the largest uncooked bird he could find.'

'Now, that really *is* an idea, isn't it?' Antonia gave a hoot of laughter as she walked back across the room to pour him a cup of coffee. 'However, you can relax.' She grinned down at him. 'Because I made the orange juice and coffee only a few minutes ago. And I reckon you're fairly safe with fresh toast and marmalade.'

'Don't go,' he said quickly, catching hold of her arm as she turned to leave the room. 'I wanted to have a quick word with you. And, since I'm not sure about the arrangements in this house, now might be as good a time as any,' he added, indicating that he wished her to sit down on the bed beside him.

Hesitating for a moment, Antonia gave a slight shrug, before slowly lowering herself down on to the mattress.

Trying to ignore the close proximity of so much warm bare flesh, now only inches away from her own figure, she suspected that Lorenzo was not, in fact, wearing anything at all beneath the thick feather duvet.

Not that it mattered one way or the other, of course. She was hardly a nervous virgin, likely to scream at the sight of a naked man. All the same...she definitely wasn't happy about the situation. Mainly because—let's face it, she told herself grimly, every single time she found herself in close contact with Lorenzo something weird seemed to happen.

Maybe it was nothing to do with him. Maybe it was all in her own head. But even now, when she was fully determined to remain cool, calm and collected, she could almost physically feel the insidious, highly dangerous tentacles of his overwhelming sex appeal slowly wrapping themselves around her nervous figure.

'I just wanted to apologise for my bad temper yesterday,' he was saying as he reached over to pick up the glass of orange juice. 'I have no doubt that if there really had been a dangerous explosion—or if it had been real gunfire, rather than those stupid fire-crackers—your action would have saved my life.'

She shrugged. 'It's all in a day's work,' she told him lightly.

'No, it's not,' he contradicted her firmly. 'You may see it as merely performing your normal duties but it was an entirely unselfish and brave thing to do.' He paused for a moment while he took a sip of orange juice.

'The fact is, Antonia,' he continued, placing the glass back on the tray, 'I'm afraid that I did not behave at all well—again. Not only was I angry and bad-tempered, but I had no right to take my resentment at the situation out on you.'

'Please—there's no need for this,' she told him hurriedly.

It seemed so strange to have Lorenzo begging her pardon that she wasn't quite sure how to deal with this entirely new side to his character.

'There's really no need to apologise,' she continued. 'Your reaction was perfectly normal. You were just in a state of shock, that's all.'

'Shock?' He glared at her. 'Don't be ridiculous, Antonia! I may have been cross and angry—but I certainly was *not* in what you call "a state of shock".'

Hah! So much for the apology! Antonia told herself, failing for a moment to see the funny side of the situation.

'OK. Have it your own way—you usually do!' she told him grimly. 'I'll try and remember that you were, at all times, as cool as a cucumber and an absolute paragon of sweetness and light. That you would *never*, under *any* circumstances, have allowed yourself to be shocked and stunned into a display of bad temper. Is that better?' she added, in a dulcet tone of voice.

There was a long silence as Lorenzo stared at her with a grim expression on his face, before giving a wry, rueful bark of laughter.

'Antonia! You are, without doubt, the most *maddening* woman it's ever been my misfortune to meet!' he informed her bluntly, his broad, naked shoulders shaking with amusement.

'However,' he added with a sigh, 'I regret to say that you are, as always, quite right. Yes, although I hate having to admit the fact, I obviously was not myself.'

'You weren't the only one,' she pointed out. 'Just about everyone else in that crowd was in a high state of panic.'

'But not you, Antonia,' he murmured, taking hold of her hand. 'You remained absolutely firm and in control throughout all the noise and furore.'

'Well…um…no, not really…' she muttered, distracted by the warm touch of his long, tanned fingers, and finding it almost impossible to ignore the effect that the sheer force of his overwhelming sex appeal was having on her pulse rate.

'No,' he agreed softly. 'Because there was a brief period when neither of us was fully in command of our emotions, hmm?'

'Yes, well, I…er…I *really* don't want to talk about it,' she retorted, her cheeks burning as she stared helplessly down at their entwined fingers. 'In fact, I…I think we both ought to forget the…er…the whole unfortunate incident. As fast as possible!' she added wildly.

'Yes, I came to exactly the same conclusion,' he agreed soothingly, letting go of her hand for a moment as he settled himself more comfortably against the pillows.

Almost sagging with relief at being let off the hook, and not having to explain her totally inexplicable behaviour, Antonia raised her head to give him a wide, beaming smile.

'On the other hand,' he drawled, slowly sliding his bandaged arm about her slim waist, 'I now find myself recalling the episode with considerable pleasure. And an even, I confess, strongly tempted to repeat the…er…the experience.'

'What...?' She gazed at him in confusion for a second, until she felt his other arm closing about her. 'Now—just a minute!'

'Well...maybe *two* minutes?' he murmured, the arms closing about her forcing her up against his bare, hairy chest.

'No...please, Lorenzo—this is a *really* bad idea!' she gasped, her senses once again totally bemused as she gazed helplessly at the warm, sensual curve of his lips, poised only inches away from her own.

But, no matter what protest she might make—or the fact that she knew, only too well, that any close contact with this man was absolutely fatal!—Antonia couldn't seem to get a grip on reality. Not when her heart was pounding like a sledgehammer, and the determined gleam in his blue eyes was prompting a sudden, deep clenching in her stomach as his dark head came down towards her.

And then, as his mouth lightly touched hers, she found herself caught up in exactly the same whirlwind of bewildering, confused emotions which she'd experienced yesterday.

Only, now...now it was somehow different. She was able to feel the exciting, erotic warmth of his naked body through her thin white linen blouse, was aware of the intoxicating, musky aroma of his smooth, hard flesh as he softly brushed his mouth over her lips, again and again, until she was almost driven crazy by a sudden, overwhelming surge of sexual hunger and desire.

As his kiss deepened and she found herself helplessly responding to the utter mastery of his lips and tongue, she could almost feel herself physically drowning in passion. It seemed as if her mind and body were slipping slowly and inexorably out of control, and she was unable to stop herself from fiercely and wantonly pressing her body closer to his, or to prevent the sound of a slight moan of disappointment as his lips left hers to trail slowly down over her neck.

But, as her eyelids fluttered open, and she found herself

almost blinded by a shaft of brilliant morning sun pouring in through the wide casement window, Antonia found herself sharply jarred back to harsh, cold reality.

'*Oh, no!*' she gasped, before making a supreme effort to pull herself together. 'I can't...I can't *believe* this is...is happening to me. *Not again!*' she exclaimed huskily as she swiftly twisted out of his arms, feverishly scrambling off the bed and staggering over to the window on legs which felt as though they were made of cotton wool.

You blithering idiot! You already knew that this guy was absolutely lethal—certainly as far as you're concerned. So allowing yourself to go anywhere near him was an absolute recipe for disaster! she railed at herself, determinedly keeping her back to Lorenzo as she frantically tucked her shirt back inside the waistband of her jeans.

Finally grabbing her courage in both hands, she took a deep breath and turned around to face him.

'Now, listen up, Lorenzo. I'm really not going to...' she began, before the man in the bed lifted his hand, imperiously cutting her off in mid-stream.

'No—I want you to "listen up", Antonia!' he said in a hard, firm voice. 'What has just happened between us is *not* the end of the world.

'Yes...yes,' he added impatiently as she opened her mouth to protest. 'I am well aware of your views regarding any close encounters between yourself and someone you regard as a client. But what we have here, *cara*, is merely a case of two people who happen to find themselves attracted to one another. A very common occurrence—and not exactly earth-shattering, hmm?'

You speak for yourself! she told him silently, since she really was feeling totally shattered by their recent encounter. But not the cool Signor Foscari, of course, she thought grimly. The damn man clearly hadn't a care in the world—leaning casually back against the pillows, and regarding her with a bland, enigmatic expression on his handsome face.

'All right...' She sighed. 'I'm prepared to go along with...er...some of what you've just said. Part of the way, at least. Because it does seem that you and I...' She shrugged, bitterly aware of her cheeks reddening under his calm, unruffled gaze as she took another deep breath.

'OK. I'll admit that I find you a very attractive man, Lorenzo,' she continued, determined to set the record straight. 'And I'm quite sure that you have any number of glamorous girlfriends back in Italy equally happy to confirm that statement,' she added sardonically.

'Ah, *cara*—I can assure you that I'm certainly no Lothario!' he protested with a slight laugh.

But she'd caught the brief flicker of his thick eyelashes, and an almost imperceptible tightening of his lips, which would seem to confirm her statement. And really, she told herself, it would be astonishing if such an attractive man *didn't* have a whole horde of girlfriends at his beck and call.

'However,' she said as firmly as she could, 'while you're under my close protection—and I would remind you that I *am* still on duty—a line *must* be firmly drawn, and maintained, between us. So, there's going to be no more hanky-panky—OK?'

'No more—*what*?'

'You heard!' she snapped. 'And don't even *think* of trying the old cliché: "I no understanda de Inglish" . Because we both know that your command of the language is probably far better than mine!'

He gazed at her with a completely blank expression for a moment, before throwing back his head and roaring with laughter.

'*O Dio...Dio!* You're absolutely priceless!' he murmured, lifting a corner of the sheet to wipe the tears of mirth from his eyes.

'Well?' she demanded, struggling to prevent herself responding to the infectious sound of his laughter as it rang around the room. 'Have we got a deal?'

'Yes, Antonia,' he agreed slowly, the amusement draining from his face. 'Yes…I can promise you that I have no intention of…how shall I put it?…of trifling with your affections. I will treat you with all seriousness and respect in future.'

'Well, OK…' she murmured as she walked towards the door. She still wasn't entirely sure that he'd got the message. But she, for her part, was going to make absolutely certain that such an incident never happened again.

Having by now got the measure of that difficult, impatient and demanding man, Lorenzo Foscari, Antonia fully expected to have her work cut out keeping him amused and entertained, during what he might well regard as a boring day in the country.

However, he and her brother Tom had seemed to hit it off straight away, getting on like a house on fire. Their friendly relations were helped, of course, by the fact that her brother had an extensive knowledge of Italian medieval history. A fact which Lorenzo, quite naturally, found particularly interesting.

She sent them off for a long walk around the village, while she prepared the Sunday lunch, and both men eventually returned with a hearty appetite.

Tom, whose tastebuds appeared to have been totally destroyed—probably from eating too many of Flavia's meals!—munched his way through lunch without comment. But she found herself feeling ridiculously pleased when Lorenzo praised the joint of roast beef, which she'd had the forethought to take out of the deep-freeze yesterday evening.

Luckily it was full summer. So, although Flavia's larder was, as usual, completely empty, Antonia had found plenty of new potatoes and fresh vegetables in the old walled kitchen garden. She'd also picked some strawberries and the first fresh raspberries for their dessert.

Antonia had once asked Flavia why she didn't employ a full-time cook and housekeeper. But Flavia hadn't seen the necessity of having someone permanently on the staff simply to make sure that their visitors had a decent meal.

'As you know, I couldn't care less what I eat,' she'd laughed. 'And as for Tom—well, your brother always has a large lunch in college, every day. Besides,' she'd added with a shrug, 'I'm far too busy to worry about such a boring subject as *food*!'

In fact, having barely contained her impatience during lunch, and hardly giving the poor man any time to enjoy his cup of coffee afterwards, Flavia dragged Lorenzo off to her studio in the converted stables adjoining the house.

Popping her head around the door of the large, airy room some time later, Antonia found him deep in conversation with her sister-in-law. They appeared to be discussing various aspects of the paintings and drawings which were normally placed in tidy racks in a corner of the studio.

Surprised to discover Flavia showing her canvases to anyone—something she very rarely did, even to members of her own family—Antonia explained that she'd just popped in to see if their visitor would care to go riding.

'It's such a lovely afternoon that I couldn't resist phoning Mike.' Turning to Lorenzo, she explained that a local farmer, who spent most of the winter fox-hunting, usually allowed her to borrow his horses when she felt like some fresh air and exercise.

'I'm not too keen on chasing after a poor fox, of course. But I do love a good gallop over the fields!' she grinned. 'However, if you two are still busy, then I'm quite happy to go off on my own.'

'No…no, I think he's probably had quite enough of me for one day,' Flavia said, smiling and thanking him for his patience, before handing Lorenzo a charcoal drawing from one of her portfolios. 'I think that's probably the best likeness. But I'd love to paint you in oils some time.'

'I should be honoured,' he assured the older woman, before gazing down with interest at the drawing in his hand. 'Yes, I agree. It is a very good likeness. I shall definitely treasure it,' he added with a smile, before strolling across the floor towards Antonia.

'You're quite right,' he told her. 'It's perfect weather for riding about the countryside. However, while I'm quite capable of handling a horse with one hand…' he glanced down with obvious irritation at his right wrist; although he had discarded the bandage, it was still not as strong as he'd hoped '…I'm not exactly wearing the right clothes.'

'We're hardly talking about the Horse of the Year show,' she pointed out with a grin. 'So those jeans of Tom's which you're wearing will be fine.'

'In that case, I'd be pleased to accompany you,' he agreed, insisting that she wait until he'd placed the drawing safely away in his room before joining her in the Porsche for the short drive to her friend's farm.

Lorenzo had been quite right, she realised some time later. Not only was he obviously well used to riding and quite at his ease astride the large, somewhat frisky horse, but, after noticing the way those strong, powerful thighs of his were gripping the animal, she had no problem understanding why he'd felt able to control his horse, despite only being able to hold the reins in one hand.

Ambling slowly along a bridle path, which ran between two fields of brilliant yellow rape seed, Antonia couldn't resist asking him how he'd got on with Flavia.

She had, of course, been dying to catch a glimpse of the drawing which her sister-in-law had presented to him. But Lorenzo, for some reason, had clearly decided not to show it to her, before putting it safely away in his room. Still, it would be an easy matter for her to take a look at it when he wasn't around.

Faintly ashamed of contemplating behaving in such a sneaky fashion, she hastily assured Lorenzo that he didn't have to be polite.

'I mean, whether or not she's any good as an artist, Flavia is terrifically successful. She's got an enormous number of clients, all queuing up to have huge portraits done of themselves.'

'I must admit to being slightly dubious about the whole project,' Lorenzo confessed. 'However, although I'm no expert, I would say that your sister-in-law was a very gifted artist. And, leaving aside her expertise in portraiture, I thought one or two of the abstract paintings, with which she's recently been experimenting, were quite outstandingly good.'

'I'm so glad that you liked her work,' Antonia told him with a broad, happy smile. 'Of course I think she's marvellous. But I'm hardly an expert. Nor is Tom, for that matter. He always just says, "That's a wonderful picture, darling. Absolutely terrific!" to everything she shows him. Maybe that's the secret of a happily married life?' Antonia added with a grin.

They rode on in a companionable silence for some moments, before Lorenzo said slowly, 'I think you're very lucky in your family.' When she raised an enquiring eyebrow, he added, 'Take your brother, Tom, for instance. I can assure you, it's been a great pleasure to talk to such a clever, erudite and caring man.'

'Caring?'

'Well, he's certainly very concerned about you, Antonia.'

'Oh, really?' she muttered, not entirely happy with the way this conversation seemed to be going.

'But yes. As far as I can see, Tom admires you enormously. Though it has to be said that he really doesn't understand and is rather bewildered as to why you should choose to have such a dangerous job.'

She gave a sharp, quick shrug of her shoulders. 'So, what

else is new?' she muttered. 'He and Flavia are always going on about wanting me to get a ''proper'' job. They simply can't understand that I enjoy doing what I do,' she added with a slight flash of irritation.

'I think you're wrong about Flavia,' he said firmly. 'She did not appear at all disturbed about your choice of profession.'

'Well, that makes a change!'

'No...' he drawled slowly, throwing her a glance of glinting amusement through his thick, dark eyelashes. 'No, Flavia seems convinced that what *you* need is a husband.'

Antonia burst out laughing. 'Nonsense! You're just making that up.'

'No.' He shook his head. 'I am, in fact, telling you the truth. Because she definitely thinks that it's about time that you settled down,' he added as they reached the end of the narrow bridle path, leading on to a lush green meadow.

'What rubbish!' Antonia gave a snort of disbelieving laughter, leaning down over her horse's neck to undo the five bar gate.

Despite being quite certain that Flavia had said nothing of the sort, and that Lorenzo was just teasing her, Antonia was nevertheless grateful that the hair falling down about her face was able to shield her slightly flushed cheeks from his view. Although why she should find the conversation about her personal life quite so disturbing she really had no idea.

Opening the gate to let Lorenzo and his horse through, she shut it again before gathering her own mount's reins in her hands.

'You go on ahead,' he said, realising that she was looking forward to a good gallop across the fields. 'To be honest, I'm still feeling slightly bruised all over, and would prefer to ride at a slower pace.'

'Are you sure you don't mind?'

He shook his head. 'No, of course not,' he told her with a smile. 'Off you go!'

Watching as she wheeled her horse about, before digging in her heels and beginning to race away across the short, springy grass, Lorenzo cantered slowly and steadily after her.

It was perhaps just as well that he had only given Antonia a brief, edited version of the long conversation he'd had with Flavia, in the studio. Nobody liked the idea of people talking about them behind their backs, he reminded himself. But it had been an illuminating conversation, certainly as far as he was concerned.

'Antonia is a wonderful girl,' Flavia had murmured earlier that afternoon, her hand moving swiftly over the pad on the easel in front of her. 'The problem is that, although she seems to be hard, tungsten steel on the surface, the darling girl is really soft, gooey toffee inside. Of course, I blame that father of hers,' Flavia had added reflectively, standing back and squinting at the charcoal drawing in front of her.

'Her father?' Lorenzo prompted quietly.

'Mmm…he obviously couldn't cope when his wife died soon after Antonia's birth, leaving him with three boys and a girl. To be honest,' Flavia admitted with a shrug, 'I can see that it must have been far easier—as far as he was concerned—to bring up all the kids in the same way. Which may have been all right when she was little, but as she grew up that poor girl never quite knew whether she was supposed to be a boy or a girl! And, to make matters worse, none of her three brothers were at all athletic or interested in sport.'

Surprised to find himself so interested in hearing more about Antonia's background, he was anxious not to disturb the concentration of the woman standing at the easel. However, he discovered that a few encouraging noises every now and then was enough to keep Flavia on track, and for him to learn all he wished to know.

'As you can imagine, Tom's father was pretty fed up to discover that his three highly intellectual sons all much preferred to keep their noses buried in a book—and weren't at all interested in playing football or cricket. So, of course, the dotty old man set his sights on Antonia—the only one of his kids who was a natural athlete, determined to try and turn her into the sort of son he'd always dreamed of having. And that, as you can imagine, led to all sorts of problems.'

'Hmm…?'

'I don't mean there's anything wrong with Antonia,' Flavia assured him earnestly. 'She's a perfectly normal, highly attractive woman. All the same, it took her a long time to grow up, and realise that there was more to life than regarding your body as a holy temple, which must be honed to athletic perfection all the time! She and I have a good laugh about it nowadays,' Flavia grinned. 'But it must have been a bit tough on the girl, all the same.'

She paused for a moment, leaning forward to make a small adjustment to the drawing in front of her, before tearing it off the pad and asking Lorenzo to turn sideways, as she wished to do a drawing of his profile.

'If you ask me, I think what that girl *really* needs is a warm, loving and happy family life, where she can relax and stop feeling that she has to prove herself all the time.

'Things would have been very different, of course, if her mother hadn't died when the girl was so young,' Flavia continued. 'She might have been able to soften her daughter's hard edge. But Antonia is so frighteningly competent and self-reliant—besides always being so *brutally* frank!— that she frightens off most of her suitors. Maybe one day she'll find a man who's sufficiently confident of his own masculinity not to find her intimidating. But quite honestly,' Flavia added with a slightly rueful laugh, 'I'm afraid that there aren't too many of that sort of man around nowadays!

'To tell you the truth, I'm a little worried about the dear girl. She has lots of boyfriends of course—any number of men who are only too happy if she's willing to throw them a glance, and allow them to wine and dine her. But she's a strong-minded girl. And, she needs to marry an equally strong man whom she can not only love but also respect. I do think that last quality is so *very* important, don't you?'

'Hmm…' Lorenzo murmured. With his Italian ancestry, he was naturally in complete agreement with his hostess as to the right and proper relationship between a man and his wife.

'All the same…' she gave a slight sigh '…I very much fear the dear girl will end up with some sort of wimp whom she can easily push around, and who won't give her any trouble. There! I've finished,' Flavia concluded, putting down her piece of charcoal and wiping her hands on a nearby rag. 'Now, would you like to see some of my paintings?'

Eventually catching up with Antonia on the far side of the field, Lorenzo thought that he'd never seen her looking so well. Indeed, with her cheeks flushed from the exercise and her enchanting, wide smile and laughing eyes, he was suddenly taken aback to realise just how badly he wanted this girl.

As they rode slowly back home in a relaxed, companionable silence, Lorenzo was only too well aware of the difficulties he faced. As he'd found to his cost, Miss Antonia Simpson was no push-over. And her obsession about maintaining a highly proper, professional distance between them was proving a considerable obstacle.

However, now that he'd decided to raise the stakes, and was hunting in earnest, he was simply going to have to find an answer to the problem.

CHAPTER SEVEN

LATER that evening, sitting in front of her mirror and slowly brushing her hair before going downstairs to prepare dinner, Antonia was surprised at just how easy and relaxed a day it had turned out to be.

What was even more surprising was the fact that Lorenzo had fitted in so easily. Neither Tom, Flavia nor herself had been given the feeling that they must entertain him, content to treat their visitor as if he were an old friend of the family.

Unfortunately—or fortunately, depending on how you looked at it—Flavia would not be cooking the evening meal, since she and Tom were attending a formal dinner in his college.

'A terrific bore, my dears,' she'd announced when Lorenzo and Antonia had returned from their ride, and everyone was sitting outside in the garden under the shade of an old oak tree, having a cup of tea. 'And poor Tom—who can resist drinking too much of the really excellent wine and port which the college serves on these occasions—*always* suffers from a really bad headache the next day.'

'It's worth it!' Tom had grinned at them, before grimacing with annoyance. 'I'm sorry, Lorenzo. I was completely absorbed in a particularly interesting piece of research this afternoon, so I forgot to say that there have been several telephone calls for you. From Italy,' he'd added, searching through his pockets, before handing his guest a piece of paper on which was written a long telephone number.

'That's odd...' Antonia had murmured with a frown. 'How did anyone know that you're staying here?'

119

'It's no mystery,' he'd told her as he'd risen to his feet. 'I am, of course, constantly in touch with my business in Milan via my mobile phone. So, if you would please excuse me for a moment...?' He'd smiled at Flavia, before walking back into the house.

'It's not important, of course,' Tom had said, helping himself to another slice of chocolate cake. 'But I don't think those calls were from Milan. I thought the man said he was calling from Rome. Still, I could be mistaken,' he'd added with a shrug, before wandering back to his study, intent on finishing a chapter of his book before leaving for dinner in his college.

'We shall, of course, be desolated to miss your magic touch in the kitchen, Flavia,' Lorenzo had drawled smoothly some time later as his hosts were preparing to leave for Cambridge. 'But I am sure Antonia will be able to whisk up something utterly delicious.'

'I wouldn't be too sure of that!' she'd told him. trying not to giggle, and wondering what on earth she could produce which would satisfy this clearly picky man.

She was still wondering if she could get away with a simple omelette, or whether to just give up the struggle and serve cold beef and salad, as she checked her appearance in the long mirror in her bedroom.

Realising that Lorenzo would still be wearing Tom's clothes, she'd chosen a very plain silk dress, in one of her favourite shades of misty blue. The loose garment fastened on her shoulders with thin shoestring straps.

It was a warm evening, and absolute bliss not to have to wear stockings, or a bra, as she'd have felt obliged to do if on formal duty in London, she told herself, slipping into a pair of high-heeled mules before going downstairs to the kitchen.

'Well! I'd *never* have believed it!' she exclaimed, standing in the doorway and staring in amazement at the sight before her.

Dressed in a pair of her brother's tight blue jeans and a freshly laundered white short-sleeved shirt from the same source, Lorenzo had a large apron around his slim hips as he stood, wooden spoon in hand, busy stirring something in a pot on the stove.

'There is no need to sound so surprised, my dear Antonia.' He turned to smile at the girl standing on the other side of the room. 'Like most of my countrymen, I take my food very seriously. Strange as it may seem, I can tell you that I am, in fact, a very good cook.'

Delighted to have the responsibility for the meal lifted from her shoulders, she grinned happily back at him. 'I certainly haven't got a problem with that. What's on the menu?' she added, coming over to peer into the saucepan on the stove.

'Nothing special, I fear. In fact—' he frowned '—I have *never* seen a store cupboard so empty. If it wasn't for the herbs and vegetables in your brother's kitchen garden, we'd be forced to go to a restaurant.'

'Oh, dear,' she smiled. 'That bad, huh?'

He shrugged. 'I'm afraid so. However, there's no doubt that you, my dear Antonia, are looking very pretty,' he said, gazing appreciatively at the girl standing beside him. 'That colour suits you.'

'Er…thank you,' she muttered, suddenly conscious of his hooded eyes lingering on the outline of her unconfined breasts. 'Shall I open a bottle of wine?' she added hurriedly, wishing that she'd chosen to wear something more decorous and formal.

He nodded, telling her to try and find a good vintage, since they would need cheering up after what would be, he assured her sadly, a very second-rate meal.

'*Well!* If that's what you call "second-rate",' Antonia said later, in amazement, 'I can't wait to see what you can produce with a full store cupboard.'

Because the meal, which Lorenzo had somehow conjured

up out of nothing, had been absolutely delicious. Starting with an improvised version of creamy cold vichyssoise—with young leeks from the kitchen garden—they'd moved on to herb meatballs made with finely minced beef, left over from lunch, in a wonderfully aromatic, fresh basil and tomato sauce—from the kitchen garden again—served with plain pasta—from a dusty packet found at the back of the store cupboard. This had been followed by fresh raspberries and cream.

'That was absolutely *wonderful*!' she assured him as he poured them both another glass of wine. 'Where on earth did you learn to cook like an angel?'

He shrugged. 'I've had one or two girlfriends, in the past, who were good cooks. And I sort of took it on from there. In fact, I find it a very good way of relaxing after a hard day's work in the office. A glass of wine, some good music on the radio...' He shrugged his shoulders again. 'You do not mind?'

'Good heavens!' she exclaimed in amazement. 'Why on earth should I mind?'

'You'd be surprised. Some women definitely do *not* like to see a man in the kitchen,' he told her. 'They seem to think that it is...' He paused, clearly hunting for the right word. 'They feel it is effeminate...not masculine, you understand?'

Antonia gave a surprised gasp of laughter. 'Oh, come on! I can think of quite a few adjectives to describe you, Lorenzo—and some of them might not be very polite!' she added, with another ripple of laughter. 'But, believe me, "effeminate" is most definitely *not* one of them!'

'Thank you for those few kind words!' he grinned, before suggesting that they take their glasses and the bottle of wine out into the garden.

'It is rather hot inside the house tonight. It will be much cooler sitting out on the terrace under the stars, hmm?'

And that was where she'd made a big mistake, Antonia told herself later.

All that delicious food, and probably too much wine as well—what had happened to her rule never to drink while on duty?—had somehow blunted her instincts and made her careless. And, sitting outside on an old swing-seat, in the bright moonlight, with Lorenzo's thigh pressed closely to her own as they swung gently to and fro, had definitely *not* been a good idea.

'The past few days have been very interesting,' he told her, gently taking the glass of wine from her fingers and placing it down on the terrace beside him. 'It's no secret, of course, that I was very much against any form of what you call "close protection"...' he added, turning to smile at her as he took hold of her hand, the shafts of moonlight emphasizing his hawk-like features. 'However, it seems only fair to say that I have, to my surprise, discovered that there are considerably worse fates in life than being looked after by the highly competent Miss Simpson.'

'If I may say so,' she murmured, feeling strangely disoriented, 'that sounds like a slightly back-handed compliment!'

She'd meant to try and keep the conversation on a pleasant, light-hearted level. Well away from any of the dangerous undercurrents which she could already feel swirling about them. But Lorenzo clearly had his own agenda. And it didn't appear to include any amusing repartee or light banter.

'Yes...it has not only been a very interesting few days, but I also want to tell you how much I have enjoyed myself today—and this evening, of course.'

'That...er...that's nice,' she said, furious with herself for sounding such an idiot—and worried about the alarm bells which were beginning to ring in her dazed, slightly fuzzy brain.

'I was telling you the truth earlier this morning,' he murmured, raising her hands to his lips. 'Believe me, I am not interested in playing games, or lightly trifling with your emotions.'

'I'm glad to hear it,' she muttered, wondering why she was still feeling distinctly uneasy.

'In fact…' He hesitated for a moment. 'In fact, I am very serious. My intentions are indeed quite…quite different.'

'I…I don't know what you mean,' she murmured evasively, feeling breathless, all her nerve-ends tingling at the close proximity of his dynamically masculine man. She was aware of a sudden clenching in her stomach at the touch of his warm lips on her fingers—the alarm bells now clanging loudly, as though issuing an imminent air-raid warning.

'Oh, yes—I think you do!' he drawled softly, smoothly placing an arm about her trembling figure and drawing her close to his chest. 'A clever and perceptive woman such as yourself, my dear Antonia, can surely be in no doubt of my desire to make love to you, hmm?'

Well! No one could accuse this man of being ambiguous—that was for sure! she told herself, having difficulty suppressing a bubble of nervous, almost hysterical laughter.

But it was no laughing matter, she realised a few seconds later. Not when his arms had closed about her, and she was now firmly trapped against his tall, dominant figure.

'OK—that's it!' she exclaimed, struggling not to give in to the temptation to rest her head against his broad shoulder. 'I thought we'd already agreed that this sort of nonsense, is strictly off limits? That this is really where I *do* have to draw the line?'

'Ah, yes—we must certainly *not* transgress the rules,' he agreed, and even in the darkness she could hear the laughter in his voice. 'But I'm confused as to exactly where we must draw this important line of yours. Does it stop here, like *that*?' he murmured, holding her still for a moment.

'Or perhaps we could extend it as far as *this*?' he added,

turning her sideways in his arms, before gently taking hold of her shaking hands and placing them around his neck.

'Cut it out, Lorenzo!' she muttered as she found herself now staring up into his gleaming blue eyes. She could feel his breath fanning her cheek, and the exciting warmth of his skin through his thin cotton shirt.

'On the other hand, maybe we could use an eraser? With a view to redrawing the line somewhere else? Like, maybe, *here*?' he murmured, his hands gently sliding down over her silky dress, slowly savouring the warm curves of her body as she clung helplessly to his broad shoulders.

'Or possibly *there*?' he whispered huskily as he softly caressed her full breasts, his action causing her fingers to suddenly tighten, burying themselves in his dark hair. She was breathless with desire, her heartbeat racing out of control.

Unfortunately, despite her stern resolve to keep their relationship on a strictly business level, she now seemed helpless, staring mesmerized up into his eyes, which were glittering icy blue in the bright moonlight. She was aware of the thick fringe of his long black eyelashes, and the slight flush of arousal beneath the tanned skin of his high cheekbones.

As the black head moved down towards her, she couldn't tear her eyes away from his mouth—descending so slowly that she was shivering with overwhelming need and desire before it softly possessed her own quivering lips. And then she was lost…lost to all sense of time and place, strangely content to cling tightly to his neck as he rose swiftly to his feet, carrying her lightly in his arms back to the house, and on up to his bedroom.

'I do not wish to hear any more arguments,' he stated firmly, lowering her gently on to the mattress. 'I am a serious man, *cara*. Not a callow youth who carelessly makes love to any woman willing to suffer his advances. You understand what I am saying?' he added softly, sitting down beside her and gently brushing a lock of blonde hair from her brow.

'I have no intention of taking advantage of our professional relationship with one another. Because that is business, *sì*? While this,' he murmured as his arms closed tenderly about her, 'this is *very* personal!'

Indeed it was! Antonia thought, shivering with tension as the sound of his deep, husky voice seemed to echo around the room. And then, as always seemed to happen when they found themselves in close proximity to one another, she found herself slipping helplessly beneath a forceful, rising tide of sexual need and desire as he pulled her hard up against his firmly muscled body, lowering his dark head to posses her trembling lips in a long-drawn-out kiss of overwhelming sensuality and passion.

Clasped firmly within his embrace, she knew that there was no point in trying to fool herself any longer. Because it was this which she'd been so desperately longing for… wanting…*needing*…ever since the first night they'd met, when she'd found herself being gripped so roughly in his arms, the mere touch of his lips having such a totally devastating, fatal effect on her emotions.

'Darling Antonia…' he muttered huskily, quickly and expertly sweeping the silk dress up over her head, and tossing it across the room, before his mouth hungrily claimed hers, the erotic seduction of his lips and tongue leaving her breathless with desire. 'I've been wanting to do this since the moment I first held you in my arms!' he exclaimed, slowly removing her panties, his hands softly sweeping up over her long legs and slim body to gently caress her breasts, the nipples hard and swollen with yearning for his touch.

And then, swiftly discarding his own clothes, he was lying beside her on the bed, his lips and fingers producing feelings of almost indescribable excitement, the subtle mastery of his lovemaking leading her gently from one delicious sensation to another, until—as if someone, somewhere, had pressed a switch—she seemed to become a completely different person, her whole body on fire with an almost incandescent, fierce longing for his possession.

Helpless in the grip of an overwhelming tidal wave of devastating hunger and desire, she felt no shame or hesitation in wantonly kissing and erotically caressing his body with a passion equal to his own. And it seemed as if Lorenzo's joyful murmurs of pleasure and delight… *'Come bella! Mia carina…mia innamorata!'*…were inciting them both to ever-increasing heights of frenzied lust and ecstasy. And then…then, as he entered her, the throbbing rhythmic movement of his body seemed to ignite a fierce flame of mutual, white-hot passion, scorching through them both with mounting intensity, until they climaxed together in an earth-shattering explosion of matchless, exquisite pleasure.

Trying to park a car in London's West End was the absolute pits! Antonia told herself, before eventually spotting and quickly zipping into a vacant parking bay.

'I won't be a moment,' she told Lorenzo as she switched off the engine. 'I live just around the corner. It won't take me more than a few minutes to collect the clothes and the other bits and pieces which I need. And then I'll drop you off back at the hotel before returning this car to the rental agency. OK?'

'No, I think I will come with you.' He grinned at her. 'I must confess to being interested in seeing your own private apartment.'

'It's really not very large. Just a simple *pied-à-terre*,' she warned him, desperately trying to remember whether she'd left the place looking tidy.

She'd only been given very short notice of her appointment as Lorenzo's bodyguard. And unfortunately she could only recall dashing around the apartment, throwing garments willy-nilly into a small suitcase, before dashing down and out into the street, to hail a taxi for Lorenzo's hotel.

'I have been sitting in this small car for too long,' Lorenzo stated firmly, his tone of voice booking no argument as he released his seat belt.

'OK,' she shrugged. There was clearly nothing she could do. And besides, even if her apartment *was* looking like a tip, she really couldn't blame Lorenzo for wanting to stretch his legs. It had, after all, been a long, tedious journey this morning, the road from Cambridge unusually crowded with heavy trucks and those monster, long-distance lorries which always seemed to clog up the fast lanes of the motorway.

Interested to be walking through an area of London completely unknown to him, Lorenzo found himself admiring the classical Robert Adam-style architecture of the buildings. And then, as Antonia led the way down a narrow street, he realised, to his surprise, that they were approaching the River Thames.

'This area between the Strand and the Embankment had seemed to have fallen on hard times before the developers moved in recently,' she was telling him, before crossing the road and leading the way into another large, classical building. But, as he soon realised, while retaining the old façade, the interior of the large block of apartments was entirely modern.

'This is very nice,' he said as she unlocked the front door, standing back to allow him to enter the small apartment. 'And it seems you have a spectacular view of the river,' he added, walking over to gaze out of the large windows at the expanse of bluey-green water, and the converted warehouses on the south side of the river.

'I only use it as a base here in London,' she told him quickly, her small sitting room—which, thankfully, she *had* left reasonably neat and tidy—seeming suddenly very small and cramped, after the huge amount of space at Tom and Flavia's house.

And, let's face it, she told herself wryly, you could put three or four rooms of this size into the large sitting room of Loronzo's suite at his hotel, and still have plenty of space left over.

'Make yourself at home. I think there's some orange juice in the fridge.' she said, waving towards the small kitchen on the far side of the room. 'I'll just go and throw a few things into a suitcase, and be back with you in a minute,' she added, going into the bedroom and firmly shutting the door behind her.

It felt very weird having Lorenzo in this small apartment of hers, Antonia thought, quickly pulling out a suitcase from one of the cupboards and opening and shutting drawers, tossing the various garments into the case as quickly as possible.

She'd only recently bought this place, mainly because it was very central, and a perfect area from which to operate when looking after her clients. Because almost without exception they were wealthy and powerful individuals who either lived in Belgravia or Mayfair, or who stayed at hotels in the same location.

The other plus was that with such little space and so few possessions she could close the front door and leave at a moment's notice—an important factor in her job, where she was often given little or no notice of an important assignment. Zipping up the suitcase, she looked quickly around the room and its adjoining small bathroom, to see if she'd forgotten anything.

Thank goodness she could always go and stay with Tom and Flavia, whenever she wasn't on duty, Antonia told herself, walking slowly back from the minuscule bathroom, having taken the opportunity to place fresh towels on the rail, already for when she next returned to the apartment.

Not having any children of their own, her brother and his wife had made it clear that they expected her to use their house as if it were her own home. And, without that safe and secure base, set within the rural English country-side, she'd probably have chucked in her job years ago. So, naturally she'd been pleased that Lorenzo, too, had seemed to appreciate the peace and tranquillity of the old Jacobean house.

Having made a valiant attempt not to think too much about the quite extraordinary, highly passionate encounter between herself and Lorenzo—mainly because, when she did so, she felt almost faint from a mass of tingling nerves and sexual excitement—there seemed nothing she could do to prevent the memories of their lovemaking last night from flooding back into her mind now.

Sinking slowly down to sit on the edge of the mattress, she found herself recalling how, time and again, throughout the long night, it had seemed as if he could not have enough of her. Nor she of him.

Woken from a drowsy sleep, she had been equally re-sponsive to the enticing excitement of his mouth moving erotically over her soft lips, immediately surrendering to the seductive, rousing touch of the warm hands sweeping possessively over her body.

Feeling weak, and even now trembling at the memory of both last night and this morning's lovemaking, Antonia realised that she must make an effort to pull herself to-gether. There were still some bits and pieces to go into her small suitcase, and Lorenzo would undoubtedly be getting impatient at having to wait so long for her to finish her packing.

On the other side of the bedroom door Lorenzo was, in fact, walking slowly around the tiny sitting room.

As Antonia had pointed out, this was clearly only a con-venient base which she used when engaged on jobs in London. There were therefore few clues as to the range of her private interests, little to give him some idea of how she spent her time when she wasn't engaged on her official, professional duties.

Why he should be surprised to see the many CDs of Beethoven symphonies and concertos—neatly stacked together with recordings of the more emotional operas by such composers as Puccini and Verdi—he had no idea. Because, if he'd learnt one thing during that quite extraordinary night of delicious lovemaking, it had been that beneath Antonia's cool, highly efficient exterior there lay a *very* passionate woman.

So, it seemed that her sister-in-law, Flavia, had been quite right, after all.

Recalling how the outwardly tough, feisty young woman had gradually softened in his arms, until she'd totally discarded the hard, steely armour with which she faced life—to disclose her intense, fiery and passionately sensual inner emotions—Lorenzo swore briefly under his breath. What was it about Antonia that he could feel himself becoming hard with arousal at just the mere recollection of the fierce, almost wanton way in which she'd responded to his lovemaking?

But there had been something else. Something utterly strange and tangible, which he'd never known with another woman. Some factor which he couldn't yet define, yet which had driven him to posses her time and again, throughout the long night.

Swearing again under his breath, Lorenzo fought for control as he paced rapidly up and down the small room, before giving up the unequal struggle. Spinning around on his heels, he marched swiftly across the carpet, and abruptly threw open the door of her bedroom.

'What on earth…?'

'My dearest Antonia,' he said, slamming the door behind him, before beginning to remove his suit jacket. 'I fear that there must be a short delay before we return to the hotel.'

She stared at him in astonishment. 'Why? What's happening?'

'There is no need to be alarmed,' he grinned, unknotting his tie and tossing it down on to the small chair in the corner of the room. 'It is merely due to the fact that I have an overriding need to make love to you. *Immediately*!' he added, his fingers swiftly unbuttoning his shirt.

'But we can't!' She gazed at him in bewilderment. 'I mean...it was only a few hours ago...earlier this morning...'

'What has the passage of time to do with it?' he demanded impatiently, moving swiftly across the room to take her in his arms. 'I want you. Right now. *Subito!*'

She gazed up at him in astonishment for a moment, before suddenly giving way to gales of laughter. 'Oh, for heaven's sake! You're absolutely impossible!'

'Is that yes or no...?' he demanded hoarsely, running his hands over the soft curves of her body.

'I think I can find a window in my diary!' She grinned up at him, winding her arms around the back of his dark head, and almost shivering with excitement as his arms tightened possessively about her.

Much later, as she lay replete against the pillows, while Lorenzo was taking a shower in the small bathroom next door, Antonia realised that she was in big trouble.

After yet another amazingly wonderful demonstration of their overriding need of one another, her emotions seemed to be in a highly confused state. Feeling distinctly not herself, and thoroughly disoriented, she nevertheless knew that she was well on the way to falling deeply in love with a man whom she'd only met a few days ago—and who would soon be returning to his own country.

And that was the crux of the problem. Everything had happened *so* quickly. And, while she hardly knew anything about this man—other than the fact that he was, without a doubt, a highly accomplished, warm and tender lover—she *did* know that there could be no happy ending to their relationship.

It was almost as if they came from two different planets—he an important businessman, heavily involved in running a large corporation in Milan, and she a bodyguard, having to drop everything at a moment's notice, and be prepared to travel anywhere in the world. What could she possibly have in common with such a man?

But that was only a small part of the problem. There was also the matter of self-preservation raising its ugly head.

Because, while she might be seriously falling in love with Lorenzo, he obviously had at least one or more girlfriends in Italy. And he was hardly likely to abandon his relationships there for someone he'd only just met here in England. And, even if she could be his only girlfriend, he obviously wasn't a man who was interested in marriage. So…this brief affair clearly wasn't going anywhere, and she'd be well advised to get out while the going was good. And concentrate on building up her own security business.

Unfortunately, that wasn't the only problem. They would, presumably, still be working together for a few more days before his return to Milan. And, however careful or discreet they tried to be, it would be almost impossible to disguise the change in heir feelings for one another—from either the hotel staff or, more importantly, the chauffeurs laid on by James Riley's agency.

She'd worked with those guys many times, on assignments like this, and they all knew each other very well. So, it was highly likely that at least one of the men—all highly trained to instantly assess a situation—would quickly sense the relationship between herself and Lorenzo. And that could have serious, and highly unfortunate, repercussions on her career.

In fact, with Lorenzo's imminent departure for Italy on

the cards, she could ill afford to take the chance of committing professional suicide.

Her thoughts were interrupted as he strolled back into the room from the bathroom, a short white towel tied casually about his slim waist. And Antonia, who only moments before had been so firmly resolved to put an end to his relationship, found her determination to do so now draining away.

His magnificent physique seemed to dominate the small room. The tanned skin covering his broad shoulders, and the muscular chest liberally covered with dark, curly hair, was glistening with tiny droplets of water from his recent shower. He looked superbly fit, powerful and overwhelmingly sexually attractive. And she suddenly realised, as a deep shaft of pain scorched through her, leaving her weak and trembling, *just* what giving up this man was going to mean.

No one died of a broken heart these days. And, of course, she'd get over him…eventually, she told herself fiercely. But, as she could almost physically feel icy cold, cruel talons hardening about her frail heart, she acknowledged that it was likely to be a very long time indeed before she recovered from the loss of this man.

Slipping out of bed and padding across the carpet to have her own shower, Antonia was further depressed to realise that, having taken the basic decision to end their relationship, she *must* force herself to do so before they returned to the hotel.

Goodness knows, she'd have done anything to put off the evil moment. Especially as she very much suspected that Lorenzo was not likely to take a sanguine, relaxed view of her decision.

It wasn't that she rated her own charms all that highly, she told herself, frowning at the reflection of her naked figure in the bathroom mirror. She couldn't hold a candle, for instance, to any of those glamorous and voluptuous women with whom, she suspected, he'd usually conducted his affairs.

However, the sudden urge to make love to her, not so many minutes ago, showed that last night hadn't been a one-night stand, as far as he was concerned. Lorenzo obviously still found her highly attractive, and would see no reason why he shouldn't be able to continue enjoying their lovemaking—at least while he was still here in Britain.

Which was why, having no problem in recalling the row in the restaurant and his loud, noisy reaction at the hospital in Cambridge, she couldn't take the risk of having such a deafening, ear-splitting quarrel taking place in his hotel, where the whole world and his wife would instantly become aware of what was happening.

Going back into the bedroom, and shooing him out of the room while she got dressed, Antonia tried to rehearse the arguments she intended to use to persuade him that it was the right decision. But, after giving herself a final inspection in the bedroom mirror, before going through into the small sitting room, she knew she was in for a hard time.

Her assessment of the situation proved to be entirely correct.

'It's no good, Lorenzo,' she told him for the umpteenth time, only too well aware of the icy rage emanating from the stiff figure sitting beside her as she drove them back to the hotel. 'You *know* that what I'm saying makes sense.'

'I know nothing of the sort!' he snapped curtly, the harsh, grating tone of his voice almost deafening within the enclosed space of the small vehicle.

Antonia gave a heavy sigh. 'You've got to face facts,' she told him firmly. 'I mean, you'll soon be swanning off back to Italy, right? And there's no way our relationship can work at such a distance. Surely that's obvious?'

'Nonsense!' he ground out. 'It merely requires some organisation on both our parts. I can easily arrange for us to still see a lot of one another. Which is why I refuse to accept for us to still see a lot of one another. Which is why I refuse to accept that feeble excuse,' he added, his voice heavy with scorn and derision.

'Oh, for heaven's sake!' she exploded angrily. 'It's simply *not* that simple. *And you know it!* Why can't you see that our relationship is like a…a holiday romance?'

'No! It is *not* like that, Antonia,' he lashed back angrily.

'Oh, yes, it is!' she retorted flatly as she turned the wheel to turn into the lane running along the back of the hotel.

This quarrel clearly wasn't going to end here. Moreover, since Lorenzo obviously had no compunction about giving full expressions to his views, as loudly as possible, it seemed prudent not to let this row continue in the main foyer of the hotel.

'Besides,' she told him, getting out of the car and collecting her suitcase, 'while I'm flattered that you don't want to terminate our affair, I've no doubt that you've got a whole harem of glamorous girlfriends in Milan. So, unlike myself, at least *you'll* be all right,' she added cattily.

'You are talking utter rubbish!' he retorted, getting out of the car and loudly slamming the passenger door shut.

However, Antonia had no problem noting the two bright spots of color on his high cheekbones, and the way he wasn't quite looking her straight in the eye.

Uh-oh! It looked as if she'd hit a raw nerve, she told herself. It looked as if he *had* got a long-term girlfriend, tucked away somewhere. So, maybe her decision to cut and run had been the right one, after all?

There was absolutely no way she was prepared to be just one of a large number of girlfriends. *No way!* she told herself firmly, her resolve stiffening by the minute as she stalked ahead of him into the hotel. And besides, she'd heard nothing during the last hour but Lorenzo's objections on his own behalf. At no point had he bothered to stop and think how it was going to affect *her*.

Bloody men—they were all the same! she told herself grimly, refusing to address another word to him until she was safely tucked away in her own suite of rooms at the hotel, with the door securely locked against the world—and Lorenzo.

CHAPTER EIGHT

THERE was no doubt that the last two days had been utterly dreadful, Antonia told herself with a heavy sigh, leaning back against her seat in the rear of the large black limousine and wondering just how long she was going to have to wait for Lorenzo?

Clearly absolutely furious at her decision to call a halt to their brief affair, the only word applicable to Lorenzo's recent behaviour was *horrendous*!

Icy cold and remote, he'd hardly been able to bring himself to behave in a civilised manner—and he certainly hadn't tried very hard. Locking himself away and concentrating on business, he'd kept as much distance from her as possible.

She had tried offering him her resignation, thinking that this would be an easy way out for both of them. But, for some perverted reason of his own, he was adamantly refusing to accept it. As was James Riley, his agency being at full stretch with so many summer visitors flying into the capital city.

So, realising that she was just going to have to tough it out, Antonia had gritted her teeth and got on with the job. Until last night, that was.

She had *told* Lorenzo—goodness knows how many times—that he must not, on any account, leave the hotel without telling her where he was going. And yet he'd done just that—suddenly disappearing into thin air, and practically giving her a heart attack, until she'd finally run him down to earth in a small bar, along the road from the hotel.

'You blithering idiot!' she had roared, her worry about his safety giving an edge to her massive loss of temper. 'I

don't know *why* I bother trying to look after you. Surely…surely you can see that wandering off by yourself, into a low dive like this, would give any assassin the perfect opportunity to knock your block off?'

'I'm sick and tired of being ordered around like a small child!' he'd snarled back angrily. 'Why should I have to account to *you* for my every movement?'

'Because I'm trying to save your rotten skin—*that's why*!' she'd lashed back furiously, finding a perverse pleasure in at last being able to release some of the stress and tension which had left her feeling totally screwed up over the past few days. 'But…hey! If you're tired of life—that's just fine by me!' she'd added with a shrill, high-pitched laugh, before stomping angrily out of the bar.

Leaning against the wall by the entrance, grateful for the darkness which was hiding her flushed cheeks, and taking deep breaths of the damp night air, she'd done her best to calm down.

'All you have to do is to tell me when you're going out,' she'd stated firmly, when he'd eventually emerged from the bar, some time later. 'I won't get in your way. I won't be a nuisance. But, I *must* know where you are at all times.'

'Yes, I understand,' he'd told her stiffly, before striding off ahead of her back to the hotel.

Antonia was well aware that she had no excuse for so spectacularly losing her own temper last night. But Lorenzo had soon found a way of taking his revenge.

Deciding to exercise her stiff limbs, Antonia opened the door of the limousine, wishing she'd had the forethought to bring a newspaper and a hot Thermos of coffee with her, like the chauffeur sitting comfortably in the front seat of the large vehicle.

'What time do you make it, Bob?' she asked, sticking her head in through the window and squinting down at the clock on the dashboard.

'It's only eleven o'clock,' he told her with a shrug, before taking another large bite from his thick cheese sandwich. 'I don't suppose your client will be out of there before two o'clock in the morning, at least. And we're not the only ones twiddling our thumbs,' he added, nodding to a long line of official, diplomatic limousines, parked nose to tail in the adjoining streets.

'Yeah...I expect you're right,' she muttered, pacing slowly up and down outside the large building in Three Kings Yard, which contained the Italian Embassy.

Every window seemed to be lit by blazing chandeliers whose light spilled out on to the pavement surrounding the building; the noise of laughter and music echoed in the night air.

Well, at least Lorenzo was enjoying himself, she thought acidly, hugging her jacket more tightly about her slim figure and trying hard not to think about the flagons of champagne and delicious food which Lorenzo was undoubtedly consuming right this minute.

She'd been on plenty of stakeouts, of course. So sitting in a car and possessing herself in patience for hours on end wasn't exactly a new experience. But she was only human. And the delight with which Lorenzo had greeted that stunning-looking girl, who'd so unexpectedly turned up to see him this morning, had left Antonia feeling sick with jealousy.

It was a terrible emotion. In fact, she was discovering, for almost the first time in her life, the utterly corrosive, destructive effect of jealousy's slimy, acid-green bile, as the evil poison flooded through the veins of her trembling body.

The young girl had been absolutely gorgeous! Unfortunately, try as she might, Antonia had not been able to discern even the slightest flaw in that perfect skin and delicate, hourglass figure. And it was clear that Lorenzo had agreed with her assessment. In fact, he'd been enthusiastically throwing his arms around the girl as Antonia had quickly decided to leave the room.

However, calling her back into his suite some time later, Lorenzo had informed her coldly that the girl, the daughter of an old friend of his, had been there to deliver an invitation. And he would, therefore, be attending a reception at the Italian Embassy that evening.

Quite why she'd been so foolish as to imagine that she was included in the invitation Antonia had no idea. Except, of course, that Lorenzo must have planned it that way. Because, as the limousine had drawn up outside the porticoed entrance, he'd obviously taken great pleasure in informing her that there was no reason for her to be wearing that smart navy silk dress.

'I really can't imagine why you wasted your time deciding which garment to wear tonight. Since you were not, of course, included in the invitation,' he'd drawled sardonically. 'Oh, dear—poor Antonia! Quite the little Cinderella, hmm?'

What was more, the swine had been clearly enjoying the fact that, furious at having been made to look such a fool, she was itching to slap that highly irritating smile from his face.

'I expect you to stay here—fully alert, observant and on guard, of course—just in case a dangerous "assassin" should happen to come by,' he'd added, giving her a cold, triumphant smile, before strolling nonchalantly up the steps and into the building.

Well, she might have known that he'd think of some way of punishing her. Because no one liked being finished with, she consoled herself. And she supposed that his rotten behaviour should at least have been predictable. But, when terminating their relationship, she'd felt every bit as much pain as he had. *She* was still wretchedly unhappy. *She* had spent most of the past two nights pacing wearily up and down, unable to gain any rest—and longing, with every fibre of her being, to be safely clasped in his arms once again.

But the fact that she, too, was in torment clearly hadn't even occurred to him. Lorenzo was totally self-absorbed in his own unhappiness at her rejection, and she could only hope and pray that it wouldn't be long before he returned to Milan.

The chauffeur's prediction was quite correct. It was just after two o'clock in the morning when Lorenzo eventually decided to leave the party.

Tired and weary, Antonia had just returned from a brisk walk around the block, in an effort to keep herself awake, and was seated on the rear seat of the limousine when she saw his tall figure leaving the building. And, of course, as she might have suspected, he was not alone.

For there, hanging on his arm and gazing adoringly up into his face, was the same girl who'd arrived at his suite with the invitation to the party.

Although she seemed to have made a mess of her life lately, that didn't mean that she was entirely stupid, Antonia told herself grimly. And when, in the full glare of the overhead porch light, Lorenzo gathered the young girl into his arms—clearly enjoying a long and lingering good-night kiss—she quickly realised that the scene had been partly staged for her benefit.

In fact, she was almost ninety-nine per cent certain that Lorenzo would have been severely disappointed if she *hadn't* witnessed that long-drawn-out embrace.

But, however much it hurt—and it most certainly did—she was determined not to give him the satisfaction of seeing that she cared one way or the other. After all, he was clearly convinced that she was a Hard-Hearted Hannah. So, why should she disappoint him?

'Isn't she a lovely young girl?' Lorenzo drawled smoothly, directing Antonia's attention to the figure blowing kisses in his wake as the limousine began drawing away. 'I really *must* see a lot more of her!' he added cheerfully, clearly gaining considerable satisfaction and pleasure from twisting the knife in Antonia's heart.

However, she'd had a few minutes to prepare her defences, and was prepared to give as much as she got.

'Yes, she really is extraordinarily beautiful,' Antonia agreed in a light, bright tone of voice. 'And clearly not a day over eighteen, either. Of course,' she added sweetly, 'if I was her father, I wouldn't be *too* keen on my daughter getting involved with a man, who must be at least twenty years older than she is. But...hey! What do I know?'

'Correct! You know *nothing*!' he grated angrily in the darkness beside her. 'You're just jealous of her youth and beauty—that's all!'

It had been a long night, and Antonia was bone-weary and fed up to the back teeth with the stress and strain of the last few days.

'You're quite right,' she said with a heavy sigh, leaning back in the seat and staring dully up at the roof of the vehicle. 'But then, that's exactly what you intended, right? So, congratulations, Lorenzo—you finally managed to hit the bull's-eye!'

'Antonia...I...'

'Oh—go to hell!' she muttered, determinedly clamping her eyes shut against the weak tears threatening to fall any minute. She *never* cried—and certainly *not* in public! she told herself fiercely, desperately striving to pull herself together.

'I fear that I am already there,' he said quietly.

'Yeah, well...that makes two of us,' she sighed. 'Only, of course, it hasn't occurred to you to even think about how *I* feel, has it?' she added bitterly. 'Oh, no—you're far too preoccupied with your *own* feelings and emotions to give two hoots about anyone else's.'

Sharply turning his head to look at the woman sitting in the darkness beside him, he was startled to glimpse tiny beads of moisture slowly trickling down the side of her cheek from beneath her tightly closed eyelids—clearly visible in the bright lights as they arrived outside the entrance of his hotel.

But, before he could say anything, the driver was opening the door, and Antonia had leapt from the limousine, quickly running through the foyer and disappearing from sight.

After yet another sleepless night—most of which she'd spent wide awake, castigating herself for being so weak and feeble—Antonia was surprised when Lorenzo summoned her to his suite early the next morning.

'I have some good news and some bad news,' he drawled blandly, his voice empty of all expression. 'The bad news is that the Rome police have apparently failed to apprehend the man who's been making threats against my life. Giovanni Parini has apparently vanished into thin air—and is therefore still a possible danger, as far as I am concerned.

'The good news,' he continued smoothly, 'is that, for various reasons, I find that I must immediately return to Italy.'

So, this is it... Antonia found herself thinking. This really *is* the last time that he and I will ever see each other. And it seemed to take the most enormous effort for her to keep standing on her feet, calmly waiting for her dismissal.

However, whatever she might have expected him to say next, she was totally astounded when he announced that he was intending to take her with him on his return to Italy.

'But you can't...' she protested. 'You don't need me. In fact, the whole idea is simply and utterly ridiculous!'

'I have already discussed my intentions with both the insurance company and Mr Riley of the Worldwide agency. They agree with me that your contract between us must be fulfilled,' he told her firmly.

'And so, Miss Simpson, I have to tell you that if you do

not comply with the terms as outlined in that contract I will be immediately suing Mr James Riley and his agency for every penny they've got. As well as making sure, to the very best of my ability, that you *never* have an opportunity to act as a bodyguard ever again.'

Rigid with shock, Antonia could scarcely believe her ears. But, as she glared up into the bland, enigmatic blue eyes of the man whom, she now decided, she loathed with every fibre of her being, she realised that there was virtually nothing she could do about the situation.

Giving a heavy sigh, Antonia did up her seat belt, waiting for take-off as she leaned back in the wide, comfortable seat of the private aircraft, and wondering just what she'd done to deserve such a fate.

In fact, ever since having been assigned to act as Lorenzo's bodyguard, her whole life seemed to have gone totally pear-shaped!

Actually, she corrected herself, it appeared to be more like one of those roller-coaster rides in a fairground. Swooshing up and down—one minute ecstatically happy, and the next thrust into the very depths of despair.

Giving herself a quick mental shake, she realised that she must do her best to try and think positively about her current situation. After all, there *must* be a silver lining to the heavy, dark clouds surrounding her. Although, for the life of her, Antonia hadn't been able to find it over the past two days.

Ever since Lorenzo had insisted on her accompanying him on his return to Milan, it seemed as though she'd been consumed by his blazing anger and cold fury. Spending hours weeping in the privacy of her own bedroom at night, and feeling exhausted and jittery during the day, she was beginning to feel thoroughly disorientated, not knowing whether she was coming or going.

Although she'd always prided herself on being a rational,

sensible human being, Antonia had never before found herself having to deal with such a maelstrom of deep, confused emotions. Could it be that despite her best intentions she'd fallen heavily in love with Lorenzo? Because, if so, as far as she was concerned, falling in love was the absolute pits!

She might have been able to cope better with the situation if Lorenzo hadn't seemed to be positively enjoying her discomfiture.

When she glanced across the cabin of the small private aircraft, her lips tightened grimly as she viewed his tall figure seated at a table fixed to the bulkhead; he was already working his way steadily through a huge file of papers.

Under any other circumstances, she would have freely admitted her admiration for his ability, wherever he might be, to concentrate his full attention on the work in hand—to be able to swiftly master a complicated, intricate problem concerning his business which would take a lesser man much longer to achieve.

But she definitely wasn't feeling fair or generous-minded towards him at the moment. And why should she, when he was clearly using his involvement in business matters to prevent all discussion of his arbitrary decision to drag her off with him to Italy?

What seemed to make matters ten times worse was the fact that Lorenzo, when he wasn't buried deep in work, appeared to have had a mystifying, *complete* change of character. Never raising his voice, he'd been scrupulously polite at all times. And, apparently fully in control of his temper—an amazing fact in itself!—he'd given her no opportunity to release her pent-up feelings of anger and frustration.

He was calm, cool, taking no notice of her tight-lipped, barely controlled rage at the position in which she found herself; it was his blue eyes glinting with amusement and hidden laughter, in an otherwise bland, expressionless face, which was mainly responsible for driving her up the wall.

Arriving at Heathrow airport this morning, Antonia had done her best to feel positive about the trip to Italy.

After her experiences with the Middle Eastern clients, trailing around various high-class shops was now low on her list of priorities. However, it occurred to her that, while in Milan, it might be a good idea to restock her own wardrobe, by visiting the designer shops and small, trendy boutiques for which the city was famous.

It was a thought that had kept her feeling reasonably content through the brief airport formalities and on to this private plane, which Lorenzo had hired for the journey.

Walking across the tarmac, he'd explained that he'd become totally fed up with regular, scheduled flights, when he'd seemed to spend far more time on the ground than in the air. Which was why he was experimenting with the hire of a private jet. If it proved successful, he might well acquire one for his company.

She had no quarrel with his decision—who wouldn't prefer to travel in comfort, rather than be squashed up like a sardine on a scheduled or chartered flight?—and it wasn't until they were in the air that she finally realised the full extent of Lorenzo's recent deceitful behaviour.

When the intercom between themselves and the pilot first crackled into life, a few minutes after take-off, she wasn't taking much notice as he ran through a list of the height and speed at which the plane was travelling.

However, she was utterly shocked and stunned to hear the pilot explaining that, with a following tailwind, their arrival at the airport, just outside Florence, was likely to be twenty minutes earlier than the normal time for the journey.

'Florence...?' She turned to glare at Lorenzo, who was busy removing a large number of files from his black briefcase. 'What on earth's the pilot talking about?' she demanded angrily. 'I thought we were supposed to be landing in Milan?'

Lorenzo merely raised a dark, quizzical eyebrow. 'Why

should I wish to fly to Milan?' he drawled smoothly. 'I can't imagine what gave you that idea.'

'But…but you said…'

He gave a quick shake of his dark head. 'I certainly told you that I was returning to Italy. However, I have no recollection of saying that Milan was my destination.'

She was silent for a moment, quickly reviewing in her memory his few references concerning his departure from Britain.

He was right. Now she came to think about it, he'd never *actually* mentioned the word 'Milan', had he? It was just that she'd, naturally assumed that he was returning to his office. And the swine had done nothing to correct her false assumption. So, what the hell was going on?

'OK…so Milan is off the itinerary,' she conceded grimly. 'But why Florence? Have you got business there?'

'No,' he drawled coolly. 'I am intending to take a few days off, to visit my old family home. And to see my mother too, of course.'

Antonia looked at him in surprise. That he should suddenly abandon his trip to England, returning as soon as possible to sort out a business problem, was perfectly understandable. But to suddenly alter one's plans in such haste, purely to visit an aged relative, seemed very odd indeed.

However, Lorenzo explained that his mother had been a widow for many years, ever since his father's unexpected and untimely death from cancer, when he'd been only a small boy. And, since she hadn't been too well lately, he wished to satisfy himself as to her general health and well-being before returning to take up the reins of business in Milan.

All of which struck Antonia as quite understandable, and she realised that there was no more to be said.

Besides, she'd heard that many Italian men, even when they had families of their own, remained attached to their old mothers' apron-strings. It was just, she mused, that she hadn't *quite* seen Lorenzo in that light.

But then, what did she know? Because nothing about the man seemed to fit into a plain, straightforward pattern of behaviour. One moment he was cool, calm and collected, and the next he could erupt like Vesuvius, in a pyrotechnic display of rage and bad temper. Was this what people meant when they talked about the Latin temperament?

Since she had no way of answering the question, and Lorenzo was currently ignoring her as he concentrated on his work, there seemed no point in trying to find an explanation for the inexplicable. She'd be far better employed reading the magazine which she'd just had time to pick up at the airport, and should just wait and see what happened when they arrived in Florence.

After an uneventful flight, they landed at Amerigo Vespucci airport in the early afternoon. However, by the time they'd cleared Customs, Antonia was feeling tired, sticky—and, above all, *hot!*

That's another thing he didn't tell me about, she thought wearily. She could feel herself rapidly wilting from the totally unexpected, blazing heat of the sun as a porter carried their bags to where a uniformed chauffeur was standing beside a long black open sports car.

'Thank you, Tommaso,' Lorenzo murmured as the chauffeur handed him the keys, before stowing away their luggage. 'At the moment, I'm intending driving myself back to Milan,' he added, dismissing the man before opening the door and settling himself down in the driver's seat.

Thanks to her job, Antonia was well used to the extraordinary way of life lived by the rich and famous. So, she wasn't at all surprised to realise that Lorenzo's chauffeur had driven the car up from Milan that day—simply to ensure that his boss could drive his own, private vehicle around the roads of Tuscany.

'Well...' Lorenzo barked, his voice abruptly breaking

into her thoughts. 'Are you coming—or not?' he asked, switching on the engine.

'It doesn't look as if I've got any choice, does it?' she grumbled acidly, her words perhaps fortunately drowned beneath the powerful roar of the open sports car's high-performance engine.

Antonia was profoundly thankful that she'd remembered to pack her dark sunglasses. She was equally relieved to note that she wasn't expected to drive his Ferrari. She definitely didn't relish the prospect of handling this powerful vehicle on the 'wrong' side of the road, and in this searing heat.

She did up her seat belt as Lorenzo let in the clutch, the car almost seeming to leap through the air as they roared out of the airport. Quickly clamping her eyes shut, she leaned back against the head-rest, muttering a prayer that they would not only arrive where they were going in one piece, but that it wouldn't be long before she was able to have a cool drink.

Lorenzo turned to grin at the girl beside him, who was looking unusually tired and weary. He, of course, loved the heat. But Antonia, with her blonde hair and fair skin, was clearly finding it a trial.

'It won't be long before we're off the *autostrada* and up into the hills,' he told her soothingly.

'But I thought...' She turned her head to look at him in surprise. 'Aren't we going into the city?'

'No.' He gave a quick shake of his head. 'It's much too hot and crowded with tourists at this time of year.'

Mentally waving goodbye to the idea of getting her hands around a long, cold drink, Antonia gave a heavy sigh. Goodness knows where they were going to end up.

However, as Lorenzo had promised, the scorchingly hot and humid conditions gradually gave way to cooler air and a welcome, light breeze as they climbed up through the hills, driving past large vineyards and olive groves.

'This is lovely countryside,' she breathed, leaning back against her head-rest, and relishing the feeling of cold, fresh air on her face. 'And what's that? It looks like an old castle,' she said, shielding her eyes from the sun as she gazed at the passing scenery on their left.

He nodded. 'It's the castle of Nipozzano, owned by the Frescobaldi family, whose vineyards produce an outstanding Chianti Riserva. They also own many vineyards and property in the region,' he explained. 'Including a vineyard at Pomino—not so far away from here—which produces a really delicious white wine.'

'I'm not a great drinker,' she shrugged. 'So I don't really know anything about vineyards and wine.'

'Never mind, Antonia...' he laughed, before concentrating on passing a lumbering old truck, which was weaving all over the road.

'As it happens, you are now in the prime wine-producing area of Italy,' he continued, when all risk of danger was past. 'So I will make sure that you have plenty of opportunity to learn more about the subject. Because I can assure you that the finest Tuscan wines are second to none!'

Antonia realised that she must have become somewhat shell-shocked by a surfeit of emotions over the past few days. Because it had taken her some time to realise that, ever since landing in Italy, Lorenzo seemed to have shrugged off the cold, icy personality with whom she'd had to deal recently. He was now once more the warm and friendly, highly attractive man with whom she'd fallen, she now realised, so deeply in love.

Was this change of heart due solely to the fact that he was back, in his own country? Or did he possess a chameleon type of personality, taking on the shades and colours of wherever he happened to be at any one time?

But, Antonia told herself ruefully, she'd been spinning around in a whirlwind of conflicting emotions ever since turning up at the London hotel to look after Lorenzo. And she no longer was certain of anything—let alone her usual good judgement, and ability to predict how people would act in any given situation.

In any case, she admitted to herself, she was sick and tired of fighting Lorenzo. If he was making an effort to be an amiable, friendly companion, she might as well respond in the same way.

'Where, exactly, are we going?' she asked.

'We're heading for my old family home in Vallombrosa, high up in the Pratomagno hills.'

'Oh, yes—I remember you mentioned it. It isn't far, is it?'

'No. The whole journey is less than an hour by road from Florence,' he told her with a smile. 'It won't be long before we are there.'

As the road appeared to climb more steeply, through beech, fir and pine woods, Antonia could almost feel the stresses and strains of the past few days slowly seeping out of her tired mind and body. The cooler mountain air was wonderfully refreshing, and she sat contentedly back in her seat as Lorenzo explained that the old house had been in his family for many generations.

'Although, of course, my mother has a town house in Florence. But she likes to open up the old family home during the hot summer months. Both I and my two older sisters and their families like to take the opportunity of enjoying a summer holiday with her. With the added bonus, of course, of being able to enjoy a cool retreat from the heat of the city.'

Taking a narrow turn off the main road, and driving slowly through a dense beech wood, he smilingly admitted that there was nothing particularly extraordinary or special about Vallombrosa. Although there was, apparently, a small modern summer and winter sports resort, just over a mile away at Saltino.

'But that's just about it—other than the monastery, of

course. You might find that interesting,' he added. 'I believe that your English poet, John Milton, stayed there for some time in the early seventeenth century.'

'What…? You mean the man who wrote "Paradise Lost"?' She turned to look at him in surprise. 'I wonder what on earth he was doing here? I didn't know that English travellers were wandering around Europe at such an early date.'

He shrugged. 'That is not an early date, as far as we Italians are concerned. Marco Polo, for instance, who came from Venice, was a great traveller, and discovered China in the thirteenth century.'

'OK…you've definitely won *that* round!' she conceded with a smile, amused by the note of pride in his voice, before he slowed down, turning the car through a wide entrance guarded by stone gateposts.

As they drove down a country track, she gazed up at the large beech trees, arching like a church nave overhead, and then they were coming to a halt in front of a very large building.

'Good heavens!' she exclaimed, gazing up at the massive walls, painted a yellow ochre colour, surrounded by tall cedars and large, brilliantly coloured shrubs and flowers. 'This isn't a house—it's practically a palace!'

He laughed and shook his head as he got out of the car, coming around to open the passenger door. 'I can assure you that it is very far from being a *palazzo*, my dear Antonia. As you will very shortly find out,' he added, before turning around to face what seemed to be a pack of noisy, barking dogs racing towards his tall figure.

'Oh, for heaven's sake! Get down, you horrid animals,' a cool English voice called out.

Antonia, who thought that she'd already had quite enough surprises for one day, could only stare in open-mouthed astonishment as a tall, slim, very elegant-looking woman with pale blonde hair emerged from around the side of the house, smiling broadly at Lorenzo.

'Darling! How marvellous—I wasn't expecting you for at least another hour. Did you have a good flight?' she was saying as Lorenzo stepped forward to give her a big hug.

It was moments before Antonia managed to get a grip on the fact that this woman—who had to be at least sixty years of age, but looked at least ten years younger—must be Lorenzo's mother.

Well! So much for the white-haired, arthritic old *mamma*!

Feeling distinctly confused, Antonia found herself being introduced to Signora Foscari, who smilingly shook her hand and bade her welcome to their home.

'I understand that you've been acting as bodyguard to my son,' the older woman said, with what turned out to be three elderly dogs running before them, as she led the way through the open front door and into a large, marble-floored hall. 'I do hope that he hasn't given you too much trouble?'

Thinking about the incident later, Antonia could only assume that she was either suffering from jet lag—which didn't seem likely—or her sluggish brain must still have been in a state of bewilderment and confusion. Because she was utterly appalled to hear herself giving a low, caustic laugh. 'Not give me any trouble? You *must* be joking!'

'Oh, dear!' His mother turned to grin at her. 'It sounds as if Lorenzo must have been extremely tiresome!'

'That's one way of putting it!' Antonia agreed swiftly, before realising, to her horror, that she was being extremely rude about this woman's son!

Hastening to make amends, she added quickly, 'I'm so sorry, Signora Foscari. I *really* can't think what's come over me.' She frowned and shook her head. 'I must apologise for being so rude. Believe me, I never meant...'

'My dear girl,' the older woman said quickly, putting a

hand on her arm, 'there's no need for you to apologise. I know my dear son—only too well!' she added with a laugh.

Smiling weakly as the sound of his mother's laughter echoed around the hall, Antonia could feel her cheeks flushing with embarrassment. She desperately wished that she'd kept her stupid mouth shut. What on earth would this woman think of her?

But, as Lorenzo entered the hall with their suitcases, Antonia was amazed when, instead of appearing offended, his mother slipped a friendly arm through hers.

'I'm sure you must be dying for a nice cool drink,' she murmured, leading her visitor out of the hall and into a large sitting room.

'Now, Antonia, I'm looking forward to getting to know you,' she added, waving towards a comfortable chair. 'So, I think we should make a start by calling each other by our Christian names, don't you? Which is why I'd be very pleased if you'd call me Sara.'

'Yes...er...Sara,' she muttered, still feeling distinctly light-headed.

'Ah, I see you two are getting to know one another,' Lorenzo said, strolling into the room a few moments later.

'Yes, indeed,' his mother said, turning to smile at him as she handed Antonia a cool glass of ice-cold lemonade, while indicating his own drink, standing ready for him on a small marble table by one of the large windows.

'I think you could even say,' she added in an amused drawl, giving Antonia a slight wink, 'that we're already well on the way to becoming extremely good friends!'

CHAPTER NINE

WITH a sigh of pleasure, Antonia leaned against the sturdy iron railings of the balcony outside her bedroom, gazing down over the wide expanse of lawn.

During the day it was a cool green oasis, surrounded by brilliantly flowering shrubs, leading to dense beech woods overlooking a steep valley, with the misty, mountainous peaks rising in the far distance.

But now, late at night, it appeared totally bleached of all colour—silvery and mysterious in the bright moonlight.

With its cool pine and beech woods, flower-filled meadows and, on the lower slopes, vineyards and olive groves, she was beginning to think that this area of Tuscany must be one of the most heavenly places on earth.

On landing at the airport she'd been hot, tired and mentally exhausted from the emotional trauma of her deeply confusing, troubled relationship with Lorenzo. But, in this peaceful house, run with quiet efficiency by Sara Foscari, she'd become aware of the nervous stress and strain slowly beginning to drain from her body.

It had a lot to do with the beautiful location, of course. But she'd also had some days of total peace and quiet, which had helped to restore her spirits. Which was clearly due to the absence of Lorenzo—who, almost as soon as they'd arrived at the villa, had completely disappeared!

He'd certainly been around when, following their arrival, she was being shown to this charming, simple bedroom by Sara Foscari. Because she'd been able to hear, despite the thick walls, the faint murmur of Lorenzo's voice talking on the phone, downstairs in his study.

'This isn't the most luxurious of our guest bedrooms,'

his mother had said, with a faintly apologetic smile. 'However, when my son informed me that he would be arriving accompanied by his bodyguard, I realised that you would undoubtedly need to be situated near him, in his wing of the house.'

Suddenly aware of a flush spreading over her cheeks, Antonia had stiffened, quickly glancing at the other woman with startled eyes. However, there'd been nothing but a bland, mild expression on Sara Foscari's face as she'd gazed calmly about the room, checking that her guest had everything she might need.

By the time Antonia had unpacked her suitcase, had a cool shower in the *en-suite* bathroom, and joined Sara in the large sitting room for a drink before dinner, it seemed that Lorenzo had vanished.

'Yes, it seems that he did have to go away quite suddenly,' Sara told her with a shrug, when it gradually dawned on Antonia that he wasn't going to join them for dinner. 'And no—I'm afraid that I can't tell you where he's gone.'

'Can't—or won't?' Antonia demanded, not caring if she was being rude. Because the sudden disappearance of her client was a very serious matter indeed.

'Ah…a bit of both!' Sara murmured with a mischievous grin, suddenly looking so like her son for a moment that it took Antonia a few seconds to pull herself together.

'Now, please understand, Signora Foscari,' she said in a hard, firm voice. 'There's no problem if Lorenzo has just popped out to spend the night with one of his girlfriends. Yes, he should have told me of his intentions before he left. Especially as he knows I'm hardly likely to be shocked by anything he might get up to. But it's not the end of the world.

'However…' she continued grimly, 'if he's taken off for parts unknown, and you *really* don't know where he's gone—or even when he's likely to return—that's *definitely* a different kettle of fish!'

'Well...I'm not sure...'

'I obviously don't need to remind you, Sara, that someone has threatened to kill your son. So, if you *do know* where he is, you'd better tell me. Lorenzo has now put me in a very difficult position. And my next step must be to start pressing the panic buttons, and contact the local police.'

'I'm sorry, Antonia, but my son did *not* tell me where he was going.' Sara gave a heavy sigh. 'I may have my suspicions, of course, but I really don't know for certain.'

'OK...but that still leaves me up a creek without a paddle, doesn't it?'

'Look, why don't we relax, have another drink, and see if we can't sort this out?' the older woman said soothingly. 'When Lorenzo left, he did promise to call me twice a day, so that we'd know that he was all right. So, why not wait and see if he phones tonight, before pressing too many panic buttons?'

Antonia looked at her steadily for a moment, before shrugging her shoulders.

'OK. I'll go along with that,' she sighed. 'But, if he doesn't ring, I'm going to be in *deep* trouble.'

Fortunately for Antonia's peace of mind, Lorenzo did phone his mother later that night. After a rapid exchange of Italian—which Antonia wasn't been able to understand, but which sounded as if his mother was giving him an earful!—she passed the phone to her guest.

'OK, you foul man—where the hell are you?' she demanded, before he had a chance to say anything.

'Ah, *cara*—relax! Surely you know that...?'

'Don't give me any of that Italian soft-soap!' she ground out angrily. 'How in the heck am I supposed to act as your bodyguard if I haven't got a body to guard?'

'I'm sorry. It was unavoidable. I've had to sort out a

long-standing problem; to settle some unfinished business. However, I have already dealt with the insurance company and Mr Riley—who have been very understanding. I will be back in three days' time.'

'Well, don't think that I won't check that out with James Riley—because I most certainly will. First thing in the morning!' she retorted, before realising that he'd already terminated the call.

'Oh, great!' she muttered, grimacing as she put down the phone. 'Now what?'

'Well...' Sara Foscari murmured. 'If what my son says is true, then why not relax and enjoy a brief holiday here, with me? Maybe a break from your duties might be a good idea?'

'That sounds marvellous,' Antonia agreed, with a grateful smile. 'Although I'll have to check up with London, of course.'

As it happened, James Riley, rushed off his feet with more work than he could cope with, merely grumbled, 'Yeah, your client has squared everything with his insurance company. No...no, I don't know what's going on. And who cares, anyway? Relax and enjoy!'

And Sara had been quite right about her needing a break from her duties, Antonia acknowledged now relishing the feel of the soft night breeze on her cheeks, out here on her balcony.

For what seemed the first time in weeks, she'd been having no problem in falling asleep almost as soon as her head hit the pillow. And, having nothing to do all day but read books or take long walks in the beech woods, she was now feeling far less stressed out than when she'd arrived here, only a few days ago.

Lorenzo had kept his word, regularly calling Sara from his unknown destination. But Antonia had declined to speak to him. 'You can tell your son that I'm on holiday— and not to be disturbed!' she'd said firmly, deciding there

was no point in having a major row on the phone. There'd
be plenty of time for that on his return!

The sound of an owl hooting down in the valley broke
into her thoughts, reminding Antonia that it was late, and
clearly time she went to bed.

Much later, as a strange sound disturbed the depths of
her heavy slumber, she drowsily opened her eyes to see the
first pale light of dawn seeping in through the open balcony
window.

'Damn owl!' she muttered, and was just falling back into
a deep sleep, when she became aware of someone slipping
into bed beside her.

Jerked instantly awake, with every nerve-end screaming
alarm, she struggled to sit up—only to feel strong, warm
hands gripping her shoulders, pulling her back down on to
the pillows. Then she heard the familiar sound of Lorenzo's
low voice, murmuring endearments as he moved to trap her
beneath his naked body, which was cool and damp from a
recent shower.

'Wh-what...?' she gasped, her brain still heavy and sluggish with sleep. 'Where...where have you been? What are
you doing here? In my room?'

'I have been dealing with a problem. Which has now
been finally sorted out. And that is the end of the matter,'
he told her firmly, his fingers gently brushing a stray lock
of hair from her brow as he stared down into her drowsy
eyes.

'Anyway—*much* more importantly—I have been forced
to have *far* too many cold baths lately! Which is ridiculous,
no? Why should I not sleep with the woman whom I have
come to love with all my heart? And who, I fervently hope,
loves me in return?'

'You...you truly love me?' she murmured, still only half
awake and not entirely sure that she wasn't, in fact, in the
midst of a rapturous, happy dream—which would dissolve
and melt away under the strong light of day.

'But of course! How can you doubt it? Surely you must know how much you mean to me? Just as I know that you have so many doubts and fears about our involvement, my darling,' he whispered thickly, pressing soft kisses on her trembling lips. 'But here, in the peace and tranquillity of my home, surely we can try to work through such problems? To build a strong relationship on the foundation of the deep feelings we have for one another?'

'Oh, Lorenzo!'

'My lovely, passionate Antonia,' he whispered huskily, his hands sweeping over the warm curves of her body. 'I was nearly driven mad when you called a halt to our love-making. Such terrible frustration! Such a deep longing to hold you in my arms, like this,' he muttered thickly, a fierce excitement scorching through her as his mouth closed possessively over first one swollen nipple and then the next.

The increasing urgency of their mutual need seemed to detonate a fiery explosion of raw passion, utterly beyond their control. Seemingly in the grip of a primitive, primeval urge to totally possess one another, there seemed no inch of her that he didn't savour.

His mouth and hands became exquisite instruments of torture, leading her from one ecstatically erotic sensation to another, and inciting her to wantonly delight in the strong, muscular contours of his body, the intimate touch of her lips and fingers causing him to groan out loud in ecstasy. And then, with a deep, impatient growl, he swept her legs apart, entering her with one fierce thrust. The strongly rhythmic, pulsating friction of his powerful body immediately ignited a mutual flame of searing intensity, until they climaxed together in an explosion of exquisite joy and pleasure.

Dazed by passion, and feeling as if she was slowly free-falling back down to earth, Antonia found herself folded within his arms, her cheek nestling comfortably against his chest as he gently stroked her hair.

'You are a very special woman,' he told her softly. 'And I regard myself as being a very, very fortunate man.'

'Mmm...' Antonia gave a happy sigh of total content-ment. 'If you reverse the sexes, I'd say Ditto...' she mur-mured drowsily, before slowly slipping into a deep sleep.

Realising that, despite their new-found happiness, she still had her duties to perform, Antonia asked Sara the next morning for permission to carry out a careful examination of the house and grounds, explaining that she needed to familiarise herself with the layout of the various exits and entrances, in case of any active threat to Lorenzo's life.

'Of course, my dear,' Sara agreed, leading her guest on a thorough and exhaustive tour of the house and grounds.

'Well...' Antonia finally sighed and shook her head. 'I think we'll just have to hope and pray that the police soon catch up with the guy who's threatening your son. Because quite honestly,' she continued with a shrug, 'I reckon this place is an absolute rabbit warren of nooks and crannies, old staircases and vast cellars. I'll probably have to call on additional help if the situation looks like getting tricky.'

'Your job sounds absolutely fascinating,' the older woman said, sinking down on to a bench in the far corner of the garden and patting the seat beside her. 'I must con-fess that I've been dying to hear all about it.'

'It's actually rather boring most of the time,' Antonia told her, before giving Lorenzo's mother a brief outline of her usual duties. She also told her about her new project, running courses to teach driving skills and simple self-defence.

'I can see that it might well be rather tedious at times. Especially looking after businessmen like Lorenzo, who we all know to be a total workaholic. Incidentally, I suppose you know the naughty man has returned home at last?'

'Yes,' Antonia nodded, carefully avoiding Sara's eyes. 'And, since he is stubbornly refusing to discuss his absence,' she added with a sigh, 'I still haven't a clue where he's been for the past few days.'

Sara gave her a sympathetic smile. 'He's exactly like his father. I loved my husband very deeply—indeed, not a day goes by, even after all these years, when I don't think about him and our wonderful, if very brief married life together,' she said softly, staring across the sun-dappled lawn towards the mountains rising in the far distance.

'However,' she added, clearly giving herself a quick, mental shake, 'my dearest Enrico was a typical Italian male. ''Never apologise—never explain'' might be their motto. Believe me, dear, they're all prima donnas!' she said with a laugh as she rose from the seat, giving Antonia a friendly pat on the shoulder, before going off to have a word with one of the gardeners, working on the other side of the lawn.

How true! Antonia thought with a grin as she walked slowly back towards Lorenzo's wing of the house.

'Where have you been?' he demanded angrily as she walked in through the French window. 'I've been looking everywhere for you.'

She gazed at him in quick alarm. 'Why? Is there anything wrong?'

'No,' he told her curtly. 'I just wanted to know where you were. You *are* supposed to be my bodyguard.'

'Even bodyguards are allowed a few minutes off duty!' she snapped. How could she possibly have imagined that she was in love with Lorenzo? He was rude, overbearing and...and utterly impossible!

'Whether you are off or on duty makes not the slightest difference when I have an urgent need to hold you,' he said, quickly crossing the floor to sweep her up in his arms.

Then, as always happened when she found herself in his embrace, with his lips moving over hers with a languorous sensuality, she was powerless to resist the instantaneous, passionate response of her own trembling body.

'Just a minute! I need to talk to you,' she muttered, suddenly realising that there was a problem that she had to raise with him as soon as possible.

'We will make love first—talk comes later,' he told her huskily.

'No...' She shook her head. 'We've got to get something sorted out. This is important!' she added hurriedly as he began pressing soft kisses over her face.

'*Nothing* is more important than the fact that I want and need you,' he told her firmly, before possessing her lips in a warm, tender kiss.

'No...really...' she gasped breathlessly some minutes later. 'You seem to have forgotten that I'm currently employed by your insurance company as your bodyguard.'

'I have no problem with that,' he drawled lazily, his eyes twinkling with amusement. 'In fact, *carina*, it must be obvious that my body badly needs your attention—right now!' he added, pulling her closer to his tall figure and leaving her in no doubt of his arousal.

But Antonia refused to be sidetracked.

'How could I look after you if an assassin suddenly appeared when we were making love, for instance? I'd be hopelessly trapped in your arms, and totally unable to save your life. And it's no good telling me to ignore the problem—because I *can't*.'

It seemed as if he was about to open his mouth and say something, when he hesitated, staring fixedly down at the girl in his arms before giving a slight shrug of his broad shoulders.

'Very well, my darling; I will accept what you say. Which means we have a problem which must be resolved, no?'

Buried in thought for a moment, he suddenly clicked his fingers. 'Yes, I think I have a solution to the problem. How about if, during the day, I am a model of good behaviour? If I am either working at my desk—or taking you out in the car, to show you places of interest in this area? And I try not to embrace you *too* frequently?

'However, at night,' he continued, 'when I insist on personally guarding *your* body, I will arrange to have security guards patrolling the house and garden. Would you find that acceptable?'

She thought hard and long for a moment. 'OK...' she agreed slowly as his arms tightened about her. 'Yes, that would probably be all right.'

'Well, thank goodness for that! Now, my darling Antonia, could I *please* ask you to concentrate on a far more important subject?' he said huskily, giving her a quick kiss, before taking her hand and leading her swiftly upstairs to his bedroom.

She wasn't, of course, entirely convinced that Lorenzo would keep his side of the bargain. And so she took the precaution of slipping silently out of his bed, very early one morning, to check whether there really were guards patrolling the area.

'You should have known that I always keep my word,' Lorenzo grunted sleepily, pulling her firmly into his arms as she slipped back into bed once more.

'Yes, well...you'd better tell those guys to get rid of those huge semi-automatics. Who do they think they are?'

'Just thugs for hire,' he murmured, rolling over to trap her soft body beneath his, possessing her mouth with a kiss of such intensity that it wasn't until the next day that she found herself wondering whether he'd been joking.

However, deciding that she *really* didn't want to know who they were or where he'd found them, she abandoned herself to the sheer pleasure of loving and being loved by Lorenzo.

The next week seemed to fly by, with each day following another like sparkling crystal beads on a string of pure happiness.

While Lorenzo was, of course, forced to do a good deal of work, he was still able to show her much of the surrounding countryside, and they visited many places of historic interest.

Florence was very crowded at this time of year, and so they only paid a short visit to the Uffizi, with its amazing collection of fifteenth-century art. Unfortunately, Lorenzo—impatient with the heat and the crowds—allowed her only a brief view of the Ponte Vecchio, the famous bridge over the River Arno, where jewellers' and goldsmiths' shops had been in existence since the Middle Ages.

'It is far too hot,' he stated firmly. 'We will come back here in September, when there are less crowds and you can see everything in more comfort. But now we will go somewhere cool for lunch, yes?' he said, before driving them to a restaurant high up in the hills at Fiesole, where they enjoyed a long, lazy meal, before returning home in the cool of the early evening.

She loved Pisa, with its leaning tower, and San Gimignano, a small medieval town, famous for its numerous towers visible from a great distance. But it was the trip to Siena, to view the Palio, which she found most thrilling.

Goodness knows how, but Lorenzo had somehow obtained seats in a building overlooking the campo, the main square of Siena—an amazing area paved in red brick and marble. And it seemed as if the whole city had turned out to watch the horse race, in which the jockeys, wearing colourful medieval costumes, paraded through the town before racing three circuits, at breakneck speed, around the square.

Lorenzo explained, as they waited for the race to start, that the Palio was, in fact, a large banner. It was for this, and the glory of representing their own, particular area of the city, that the riders were prepared to risk the lives of themselves and their horses.

With the excitement mounting, minute by minute during the late afternoon—the air filled with the sound of trumpets, and the noise of a huge crowd of people, all cheering on their favourites—Antonia found herself totally caught up in the atmosphere.

They arrived back at the house late that night, and it wasn't until the next morning, at breakfast, that she learned of the large family luncheon party to be held later that day.

Not sure how she felt about meeting all of Lorenzo's family *en masse*, Antonia suggested that perhaps it might be a good idea if she made herself scarce.

'I'd quite like to see that old convent,' she told Sara. 'And I could maybe take a picnic with me, and...'

Nonsense! Of course you must join us,' Sara told her firmly. 'And besides, my daughter Claudia wants to meet you,' she added, her eyes twinkling with amusement. 'Something to do with a pair of earrings?'

'Oh, Lord!' Antonia groaned. 'I'd forgotten all about that. I hope she wasn't cross about it?'

'No, of course not!' Sara laughed. 'She was merely intrigued to hear my granddaughter telling her about Uncle Lorenzo's new girlfriend.'

Suddenly kicking herself for not having realised that this very astute, clever woman must of course be well aware by now that she and Lorenzo spent each night locked in each other's arms, Antonia couldn't seem to stop a deep flush from rising up over her cheeks.

What on earth did you say to a man's mother, under these sort of circumstances? she wondered wildly. But, if Sara Foscari had any thoughts on the matter, she was keeping them firmly under wraps, calmly pouring herself another cup of coffee, before changing the subject and asking Antonia whether she'd enjoyed the Palio.

Later in the day, as Antonia gazed at herself in her dressing-table mirror, wondering whether her simple pale blue cotton dress was perhaps just a little too casual for a formal family meal, she couldn't help feeling nervous about meeting Lorenzo's family.

However, later, as she sat among the throng of happy,

noisy relatives, Antonia realised that she needn't have worried. Everyone was very friendly. Especially Claudia—the plump, dark-haired mother of Maria, whom she'd met in Cambridge.

Claudia introduced her to Lorenzo's other sister, Isabella—a complete contrast to Claudia, being blonde and slim like her mother.

The only strange note about this lunch was the fact that Lorenzo's mother was casting her son occasional, anxious glances, and not appearing her usual calm, relaxed self. In fact, Antonia told herself with a slight frown, Lorenzo had seemed slightly edgy and ill at ease ever since receiving a phone call from Milan, earlier this morning.

Maybe it was business problems, she told herself with a shrug, her thoughts interrupted as, with the noise of much laughter and the loud ringing of knives being tapped against the large wine glasses, she saw Lorenzo rising slowly to his feet, at the other end of the table.

Speaking in Italian, of course, of which she caught only a few words, including her own name, he eventually paused, amidst the sound of much laughter, and turned to face her.

'I have been telling my family, Antonia, the reasons why it was necessary that I should be provided with a bodyguard. And how astonished I was—and maybe not too happy, either—to have a woman telling me what I could and could not do. However, I have now reassured my family that I am a reformed character, and clearly understand the necessity of doing as I am told—at all times!'

'Quite right!' Claudia laughed, before turning to wink at Antonia. 'And, if you have any nonsense from my little brother, just let me know. I'll soon sort him out!'

Her 'little brother', who stood well over six foot, joined in the general laughter. As the meal drew to a close, and the assembled company broke up into various groups, Sara Foscari announced her intention of taking a short nap.

Lorenzo appeared engrossed in an animated discussion with his two brothers-in-law about national politics—and many of the younger members had decided to play football on the large lawn.

Which led Antonia to decide that this might be the right moment to slip away.

Picking up her handbag and slowly making her way from the vine-covered patio into the house, she was stopped by one of the servants, conveying the message that someone wishing to see 'the English lady' was waiting in a small salon, at the end of the corridor.

Mystified as to who would want to see her, Antonia opened the door, surprised to see standing by the large window in the salon a woman whom, she was quite certain, she'd never seen before in her life.

'Well...hello!' the stranger murmured, turning to face Antonia as she closed the door behind her. 'We haven't met before, of course,' the woman added with a brief, flickering smile. 'But you must be dear Lorenzo's bodyguard?'

'Er...yes, I am,' she murmured, wondering exactly where this exquisitely beautiful woman fitted into the family.

'And also, I understand, his new girlfriend?'

'Well...er...' Antonia muttered, her mind racing as she tried to work out how to answer such a blunt question. After all, the fact that she and Lorenzo were sleeping together was entirely their own business. And he certainly hadn't gone public with his own family, right? So, if this woman was a relative of his, it might be as well to tread very carefully.

'I'm sorry, I didn't catch your name. You are?'

The woman stared silently at her for a moment, before giving a long, slow smile.

'How remiss of me not to introduce myself,' she murmured. 'However, for your information, my name is Gina Lombardi. And I was, until a few days ago, engaged to be married to Lorenzo Foscari.'

Feeling totally confused, with thoughts and questions buzzing noisily in her brain, like wasps trapped in a jam jar, Antonia could only stare speechless and dumbstruck at what had to be one of the most beautiful women she'd ever seen.

But then, as she gradually pulled herself together, the full import of what the stranger had said gradually became clear.

Gina? Gina Lombardi? Yes, of course! This *must* be the woman whom Giles Harding's wife had referred to, so disparagingly, during the interval at the Albert Hall—the evening when she'd first been appointed as Lorenzo's bodyguard.

Her memory of that night, and who had said what to whom, was a little hazy. But Antonia now recalled her distinct impression that Mrs Harding had actively disliked Gina.

Which wasn't surprising, Antonia told herself, after another swift glance at the woman, who was now admiring her reflection in a large gilt mirror on the wall by the window.

Such a perfect face and figure was guaranteed to make *any* normal female feel highly depressed about her own appearance. And she, herself, wasn't exactly feeling *too* happy at the moment, either.

Of medium height with slim legs, perfect ankles and a voluptuous, sexy figure positively guaranteed to make strong men weep, Gina had classical features and an utterly flawless complexion, surrounded by a mass of dusky curls, tumbling seductively down about her shoulders. Although possibly older than she looked, Antonia had not the slightest doubt that this woman had only to beckon with one of her little fingers at any normal, red-blooded man— to have him lying panting at her feet, in five seconds flat!

Beginning to recover from her shock at Gina's sudden appearance, Antonia realised that she had a potentially very tricky situation on her hands. Especially if this exquisitely beautiful woman really *was* Lorenzo's ex-fiancé. And quite how she was going to handle it she had no idea.

However, having brushed a hand through her shiny dark curls, and made a slight adjustment to the skin-tight silk dress, clinging like a limpet to her outstanding figure, Gina clearly had her own agenda in mind as she turned around to face Antonia.

'Lorenzo's such an attractive and charming man, isn't he? And amazingly talented in bed, too, of course,' she added, another small smile playing around her lips. 'There's no doubt that I'm really going to miss him.'

'I'm sorry,' Antonia shrugged. 'But I really don't see that this is anything to do with me. If you've got a quarrel with Lorenzo, then I suggest that you take it up with him.'

The beautiful woman shook her head. 'No, I've no quarrel with dear Lorenzo—oh, dear me no. So kind. So very, very generous,' she murmured, gazing down at her beautifully manicured hand, and admiring the spectacularly large, flashy diamond ring on one of her fingers.

'No...' she cooed, raising her large dark eyes to gaze over at Antonia. 'I'm only here because...well, I'm a great believer in female solidarity.'

Female solidarity—my foot! Antonia told herself, convinced that this amazingly good-looking woman would have had as little to do with other females as possible.

Glimpsing the highly sceptical expression on Antonia's face obviously prompted Gina to change tack.

'Well...maybe I was putting that just a little strongly,' she admitted with a shrug. 'But I thought it only fair to come and tell you that if you're hoping that Lorenzo is going to marry you you're very much mistaken.'

'I can assure you that the question of marriage to Lorenzo—or anyone else, for that matter—has simply not crossed my mind,' Antonia informed her coldly.

'Oh, don't be silly, darling!' Gina waved one of her

hands briskly in the air. 'As soon as a woman falls in love with a man—of course she's planning to marry him. Which is precisely why I'm here. To save you a great deal of unhappiness and heartache. Because I'm afraid that, whatever he might say, Lorenzo has absolutely no intention of marrying you. Believe me,' Gina told her coolly, 'I know what I'm talking about. Dear Lorenzo has a really big problem when it comes to telling the truth.

'For instance,' she continued, 'I wonder if he's told you that he spent three days in bed with me only last week, when he visited Milan? Oh, no—I can see he didn't,' she murmured, clearly enjoying the expression of shock on Antonia's face. 'Never mind, dear, I expect he told you it was just business—right? But that was just another one of his little lies, like promising that we were to be married. And why not, when I had been his wife in all but name for the past year?'

Determinedly ignoring the shaft of pain zigzagging through her at the thought of Lorenzo making love to this woman, Antonia took a deep breath to steady herself. She had to cling to the thought that Lorenzo's private and personal life, before they'd met and fallen in love with one another, was nothing to do with her. Although the information that while she and his mother had been worried about his whereabouts for those missing three days he'd been in bed with this awful woman was desperately hurtful—and not something that she could cope with at the moment.

'Look, I don't know the ins and outs of this situation,' Antonia said, determined not to let Gina realise just how upset she was about that episode in Milan. 'But these things do happen. People can change their mind. And surely it's better to do so rather than making the mistake of marrying the wrong person?'

'Yes, that sounds very reasonable,' Gina nodded, turning to view herself in the mirror once again. 'And you are undoubtedly thinking that, even if he lied to me, there's no reason to believe that he would treat you in the same way. Yes?'

Antonia shrugged.

'Unfortunately, the lies he has told me are *nothing* when compared to the deceit which he has practised on *you*. And, what is more, I can prove it,' Gina told her as she walked over to the small table by the window, where she'd left her handbag. 'My friends in Milan tell me that you are here as Lorenzo's bodyguard. Correct? To look after him because of the threats against his life made by Giovanni Parini?'

Antonia nodded. 'Yes, you're quite right,' she said, wondering how this woman had discovered that fact. Could some of the guards, recently appointed by Lorenzo, have been opening their mouths in the local bars? It seemed as though she'd hit the nail on the head when the other woman gave a low chuckle of laughter.

'I can assure you, we've all had a great deal of amusement from the situation. Everyone is saying; Why should Lorenzo need a bodyguard? Especially when Giovanni Parini was caught over two weeks ago, and has been in a police cell ever since.'

'*What*? What did you say?'

'Here—see for yourself!' Gina laughed, walking over to hand the newspaper cutting to Antonia.

It was in Italian, of course, so she had difficulty in reading the report through in its entirety. However, there was the picture, clearly captioned with his name, of Giovanni in handcuffs with a policeman's hand firmly placed on his shoulder, as he was being escorted into what looked like a police station.

However, Antonia's relief at realising that the possible assassin was now well and truly under lock and key soon faded away as she noted the date printed at the top of the newspaper.

Oh, my God! This awful woman was quite right, Antonia

told herself, Remembering Tom telling Lorenzo about his calls from Italy and realising that the man must have been apprehended on the very day when she and Lorenzo had visited Cambridge. Which meant…yes, it *had* to mean that Lorenzo must have known *before* his sudden decision to return to Italy that his life was no longer in danger.

'You see!' Gina exclaimed, a note of triumph in her voice. 'I told you he was a liar—didn't I?'

'Yes…Yes, you did,' Antonia whispered, utterly shocked and stunned as she stared uncomprehendingly down at the piece of paper in her hands.

Why? *Why* had Lorenzo done this to her? Why had he continued to pretend that he was in danger—when he was nothing of the sort? Oh, Lord—she was going to be the laughing stock of her profession! No one would *ever* let her forget that she'd been so much in love with a man that she'd continued his 'close protection' when there'd been absolutely no need for her to do so!

Almost gasping with pain, she staggered over to sink down into a small chair, with Gina's hateful, caustic laughter ringing in her ears.

As she buried her face in her hands, Antonia's mind was totally filled by two questions, which kept repeating themselves in a continuous loop through her brain: *How could he have done this to her? And what was she going to do now?*

CHAPTER TEN

CLICKING her teeth with annoyance, Antonia glanced down at the watch on her wrist. She wasn't going to wait much longer. If the stupid man didn't turn up for his appointment fairly soon, she was going to call it a day, lock up her office here at the airfield, and drive back to London.

These chauffeurs were all the same! They hated anyone telling them how to drive their boss's car. And unfortunately, since most of them were middle-aged, retired police drivers, they bitterly resented being given instructions by a mere woman.

With a heavy sigh at the realisation that nothing seemed to be going right for her lately, she tried to concentrate on the pile of papers in the file on her lap. But, as so often happened nowadays, it seemed almost impossible to keep her mind on anything.

Although she'd hoped that, after six weeks, the events in Tuscany would have begun to fade slightly from her mind, nothing of the sort seemed to have happened.

Sitting there in Lorenzo's family home, that awful afternoon, totally shattered and dazed with bewilderment, she'd desperately tried to think what she was going to do about the situation.

But she'd soon realised that she needed to get away. To think things through, in peace and quiet. And without that awful woman's laughter ringing in her ears.

'For goodness' sake—shut up!' she'd growled angrily at Gina, who'd fallen silent as the tall Englishwoman had begun pacing up and down the floor, clearly buried deep in thought.

Realising that it wouldn't be long before they were disturbed by a member of the family—and she *really* didn't want to see Lorenzo at this point—Antonia had turned abruptly on her heels to face Gina.

'You live in Milan, don't you?' When the other woman nodded, she demanded, 'So, how did you get here today?'

Gina shrugged. 'I just caught a plane to Florence, and hired a car at the airport.'

'Right!' Antonia muttered, quickly walking across the room and seizing up Gina's handbag, rooting through it for the keys to her car.

'What are you doing? Where do you think you're going?' Gina cried as Antonia turned swiftly towards the door. 'You can't just steal my car and leave here, without a word!'

'You've got a point,' Antonia muttered, quickly halting and retracing her steps to pick up the large newspaper cutting. After slipping it under the top edge of the mirror on the wall, she grabbed a lipstick out of her own handbag, quickly printing, *'I THINK THIS SAYS IT ALL!'* in large capital letters on the glass.

Realising that she couldn't take the risk of leaving Gina behind, since the other woman would undoubtedly tamper with the message she'd left for Lorenzo, Antonia quickly took hold of her arm, dragging her reluctant figure towards the door.

'What do you think you're doing? Take your hands off me—at once!' Gina protested loudly.

'Shut up!' Antonia hissed savagely. 'If I have one more peep out of you, I'll leave you here, trussed up like a chicken! So, just behave yourself and do as I say.'

Her threat, which she would never, of course, have carried out, proved effective, clearly frightening Gina into doing as she was told.

And nothing is ever wasted, Antonia told herself grimly, grateful that she'd taken the time to go over this huge house inch by inch, when determined to ensure Lorenzo's protection and safety. While she now knew *that* effort had been a total waste of time, it did enable her to frog-march Gina down a small, dark corridor and out of a door at the side of the house not normally used by the family.

Locating Gina's small Fiat parked under some nearby trees, Antonia shoved her into the passenger seat, before taking her own place behind the wheel, switching on the engine and roaring off down the drive.

There wasn't any clear plan of action in Antonia's mind when she left the villa so precipitously. She only knew that she had to get away for a while—and to put some distance, however temporary, between herself and Lorenzo. She also knew that it was unlikely that she would be missed for at least the next hour or so. Which would give her time to think through, clearly and objectively, the whole situation. And, above all, to try and understand *why* Lorenzo hadn't told her about the arrest of Giovanni Parini.

The woman sitting beside her was clearly not happy as Antonia drove the car fast down the mountainside—gasping out loud in terror as the small Fiat seemed to take the hairpin bends on only two wheels.

'Where…where are we going?'

'I've no idea,' Antonia snapped curtly. 'Where does this road lead to?'

'Florence,' Gina muttered in a small voice.

And it was then that Antonia realised that she had her passport and credit cards in her handbag, which she'd taken with her on leaving the patio.

And, since she didn't want to have anything to do with Lorenzo—not until she'd really thought the whole problem through—there was clearly no point in hanging around here, in Italy. Especially as he'd have no problem in tracking her down. In fact, probably her best option would be to try and put as much distance between them as possible.

Which was why, after demanding that Gina direct her to

the airport, she found herself boarding a plane back to Britain.

But now, over six weeks later, she was no nearer coming to a real understanding of why Lorenzo had behaved the way he had. And even going to stay with Tom and Flavia had proved to be of small comfort.

'It's no good expecting me to answer such a complicated question,' Flavia had muttered when, for the umpteenth time, Antonia had demanded an answer to her problem. 'Men are complicated creatures at the best of times,' her sister-in-law had added, mixing some paint on her palette before leaning forward to complete the background to a still life on the easel in front of her.

'The thing is,' Antonia had said, pacing up and down the large, airy studio, 'even if that awful woman Gina was lying through her teeth, there's still the problem of *why* Lorenzo didn't tell me that he was no longer in danger.

'After all,' she'd added, 'I didn't have any other jobs lined up. He could have said, "They've got hold of the bad guy. So let's go off and have a holiday with my mother." Why invent a whole tissue of lies?'

'I honestly don't know, dear,' Flavia had murmured. 'I do remember thinking that he was absolutely dotty about you, if that's any help. After all, he did ask for one of those drawings I did of you last Christmas.'

'What?' Antonia had frowned at her. 'What on earth are you talking about?'

Flavia had shrugged. 'It was when you came here—after the explosion. I was drawing him…such a magnificent head…and then he asked to see some of my paintings.'

'So?'

'So, when he particularly admired one of the drawings I'd done of you, I gave it to him,' she'd explained. 'As I said—he seemed very keen on you. At the time, anyway.'

Antonia had given a heavy sigh. 'Yes, I think he was—at the time.'

'And I'm sure he still is,' Flavia had told her firmly. 'But you know what people are like when they're in love. All rational thought and logic seem to fly out of the window. Quite honestly, darling,' she'd added, standing back to take a good look at her work, 'I can't help thinking that the easiest and quickest way to answer all your questions would be to ask Lorenzo himself.'

Flavia hadn't seemed to understand why she *couldn't* bring herself to do that. Unfortunately Antonia knew, with absolute certainty, that she'd only have to hear that low, sexy voice for all her strength and resolution to immediately dissolve and melt away. And, having fallen so deeply in love with a man who appeared to have no trouble in charming the birds from the trees, she knew that she would be nothing but putty in his hands.

Besides, she told herself angrily, he hadn't made the slightest attempt to contact *her*, had he? In fact there'd been a deafening silence, as far as any contact with Italy was concerned.

There had been, of course, many times when she'd almost weakened. Those moments during the small hours of the night, when she'd woken to find her pillow damp with tears, the temptation to pick up the telephone had been almost irresistible. But she *had* conquered the impulse, her resolution hardening whenever she thought about Lorenzo and Gina.

Because, of course, that hadn't been something that she'd felt able to discuss with her sister-in-law, Flavia. How could she admit to the searing, corrosive green jealousy which left her weak and trembling with pain whenever she thought about Lorenzo making love to such a spectacularly beautiful woman? There were even times, huddled in her lonely bed, when she found herself whimpering out loud with agony, tortured by flickering images of him intimately caressing the other woman's body.

Because, while she might have made a fool of herself

over Lorenzo, she wasn't entirely an idiot. She knew that Gina must have come to the villa specifically to wreck her involvement with Lorenzo. And, having successfully achieved her aim, the other woman would undoubtedly have done all she could to entice Lorenzo back into her bed. And what man could possibly resist such perfection?

The only faint light on the horizon concerning this whole, wretched affair was the fact that the news didn't seem to have got out amongst her profession. No one seemed to realise, as yet, that she'd been made such a fool of by Lorenzo. That was undoubtedly due to the fact that this was one of the busiest times of the year for those involved in close protection. But Antonia feared that it could only be a matter of time before James Riley, at least, would have no problem in putting two and two together. And that was hardly a prospect to be relished.

With another heavy sigh, Antonia tried to concentrate on filling in the time sheet in front of her. What was this guy's name? She turned over a piece of paper to check his details. Well, if Eric Chapman, whoever he was, didn't put in an appearance soon, she was going to send him off with his tail between his legs. And then have a few hard words with his boss! she was telling herself irritably when there was a knock on the door.

'Come in,' she barked, refusing to look up and continuing to tick the boxes on the form in front of her, in order to teach the man a lesson.

'You cannot allow your employers to pay for a course, and then turn up a good half-hour late. Please sit down,' she continued, still keeping her eyes firmly down on the work in front of her. 'I just have to finish filling in these forms.'

There was a sound of a chair being pulled up to the desk and a low rumble of laughter as the man sat down before her.

'I'm afraid that I don't find your lack of punctuality quite so amusing,' she was saying as she raised her head to glare angrily at the man. 'In fact, I've a good mind to... *What the hell...*!' She gasped, staring transfixed into the face of Lorenzo, sitting only a foot or two across the desk.

'What...what the heck are you doing here?' she whispered, when she'd at last managed to find her voice.

He gave a shrug of his broad shoulders. 'One of us had to break the silence, Antonia,' he drawled smoothly.

'Oh—right! And that's it?' she demanded incredulously. 'No other explanation? No reason for not getting in touch with me for six weeks?'

He gazed at her steadily for a moment. 'I now find myself wondering why I have bothered to make the effort to contact you,' he told her sternly. 'After you demonstrated such a total lack of trust...the distress you have caused me... Believe me, Antonia, there have been times when I *never* wished to see you again!'

'Hah—that's rich!' she snapped. 'And what about *my* distress? What about the fact that you *lied* about Giovanni Parini being still dangerously on the run, when you blackmailed me into going with you to Italy? The *lies* you must have told those hoodlums, protecting a man who already knew he was quite safe. And what about the fact that you're probably going to make *me* the laughing stock of my profession?'

To her utter astonishment, he merely shrugged his shoulders.

'Well?' she demanded angrily. 'Don't you think that I am at least entitled to an explanation?'

'And how, my dear Antonia, am I supposed to explain one of the great mysteries of life? How can I, a mere mortal, give you a definitive explanation as to why two people fall in love?'

'I...I don't know what you're talking about,' she muttered, so used to Lorenzo's fiery, emotional response to any difficulty in his path that she now found herself feeling totally confused—and badly frightened.

Because she very much feared that Lorenzo hadn't come here gripped by a passionate desire to reclaim his new girl-friend—as, to be entirely honest, she'd been hoping and praying that he would. And, whatever the reason for his appearance, she had an awful feeling that this meeting was definitely not going to end on a happy note.

Suddenly not able to bear the fact that the one and only man she'd ever truly loved was now sitting only a few feet away, and regarding her with such cold, dispassionate eyes, she quickly pushed back her chair. Rising to her feet, she moved swiftly across the small office, towards a window on the other side of the room.

'Yes, I realise that you do not know what I am talking about, Antonia,' he told the woman now standing with her back to him, her figure stiff and rigid as she stared out of the window. 'So, how can I hope that you will understand the force of the love I had for you, hmm?'

With every sense acutely aware of the man sitting at his ease behind her, Antonia immediately picked up the fact that he was using the past tense when describing his feel-ings for her.

So, that was why he was here. To tell her that it really *was* all over between them. Well…she'd just have to take it on the chin. Stand firm. Let him think that she didn't give a damn. Goodness knows, there'd be plenty of time to weep her eyes out after he'd gone. The rest of her life, in fact.

'You have accused me, quite correctly, of lying to you about Giovanni Parini,' Lorenzo said, his voice seeming to come from a long way off as she struggled to hold herself together. 'You are also quite right when you say that I used threats to force you to accompany me to my home in Tuscany. Moreover, I have no wish to deny that I went through the farce of hiring guards when I knew that I was perfectly safe.

'In fact, my dear Antonia,' he added quietly, 'I freely admit that you are right to accuse me of deplorable conduct towards you. On that, at least, we can agree.'

'But why? *Why?*' she muttered, still staring blindly out of the window, desperately trying to control the weak tears threatening to fall any minute, and almost choking on a hard lump which seemed to have become stuck in her throat.

'Ah—now *that* is the point at issue,' he said, before giving a heavy sigh. 'Although I'm not sure I can fully explain the power of love. Because, you see, although I fought it like the devil, I *did* fall very suddenly and violently in love with you. And I then discovered, admittedly rather late in life, that real, true love is an all-consuming emotion.

'So, there really is no easy explanation of *why* I did what I did. Possibly the unpleasant truth, my dearest Antonia, is that when you decided our affair was over I discovered—to my horror, I may say—that I was prepared to lie, cheat, steal…just about anything, other than murder, of course…to keep you by my side, until such time as I could persuade you of my deep feelings—persuade you that, if we *truly* loved each other, as I believed we did, we *could* have a future together.

'But you…you never gave us a chance. In fact, your total lack of faith and trust in me was truly abysmal. At the first sign of difficulty, you immediately took to your heels and ran away, didn't you, Antonia?' The harsh contempt in his voice caused her to gasp, as though she'd been wounded by a savage blow to her solar plexus.

'However, there's no doubt I should have called a halt to the farce,' Lorenzo admitted with a heavy sigh. 'Which I planned to do after the lunch my mother gave to introduce you to the family.'

'To introduce *me*?' she muttered, her mind in a complete state of confusion. 'But I thought…'

'Why else would my family make an effort to come so

far—unless they had suspected that I wished to introduce them to the woman I intended to marry?'

'But...but you never said anything about wanting to marry me,' she said, turning slowly around to face him.

He shrugged. 'I was intending to ask you, after lunch. But then you ran away, didn't you, Antonia? Why did you listen to that stupid woman's lies? Oh, yes—I realised that it must have been Gina who'd called to see you that afternoon. The servants had no problem in describing her very accurately,' he added caustically.

'Yes, well...that's another thing!' She scowled at him. 'How about those three days in bed with lovely Gina? It sounds like you had a high old time in Milan, leaving me to worry myself sick about your safety! How could...how *could* you come straight from that awful woman's bed to mine?' she cried, tears of anger and frustration filling her large grey eyes.

'Ah, my darling!' he murmured, rising swiftly to his feet and striding quickly across the room to take her in his arms. 'How can you imagine...how can you possibly believe that I would do such a thing?'

'But Gina said...and even your mother seemed to know where you were...and I was so worried about you,' she muttered tearfully, burying her head in the curve of his shoulder as his arms closed protectively about her.

He gave a heavy sigh, before leading her tearful, trembling figure over to a sofa on the far side of the room.

'My mother is a clever and astute woman,' he said, sitting them both down on the soft cushions. 'So, of course, she would have had a very good idea of where I was going—and what I intended to do, before my return to you, at the villa,' he added, placing a hand firmly beneath Antonia's chin and tilting her face up towards him.

'I told you, the first time we made love together, that I was a serious man—yes? And that means that I did not feel I could...that I was not at liberty to tell you of my deep love for you while there was even the slightest question of another woman in my life. And so, although my relationship with Gina Lombardi had come to an end before I met you, I had to make sure—for the sake of my own honour if nothing else—that she was both well provided for and that I had definitely closed that chapter of my life, before I could begin a new one, with you. Do you understand what I'm saying, Antonia?'

She nodded.

'So, as soon as we arrived at my home in Vallombrosa, I immediately drove to Milan to sort out Gina, buy her an apartment, some trinkets and a new car, before returning with a clear conscience to tell you how much I loved you and hoping to ask you to be my wife.'

'And…and you weren't *really* engaged to Gina?'

'Of course not!' He waved a hand dismissively in the air. 'I may have…er…enjoyed her company in the past. But I was never in love with her. So how could I possibly have asked her to marry me?'

'I'm sorry…I should have trusted our love for one another, shouldn't I?' she muttered, brushing the tears from her eyes. 'But I still don't see why…I mean, you must have known how upset I'd be when I found out that you'd been lying about needing a bodyguard, once Giovanni Parini was in custody? So…so why didn't you get in touch with me before now?'

'My darling, I've not been able to see you before now because my mother had a sudden heart attack, only a few days after you ran away.'

'*Oh—no!*' Antonia cried, gazing at him with horrified eyes, all their problems and her differences with Lorenzo completely forgotten in her overriding concern for a woman of whom she'd become so fond. 'I'm *so* sorry. I know just how important she is to you. Is…is she going to be all right?'

He nodded quickly. 'Yes, it was only a mild attack. A warning to take it easy.'

But when she remained clearly upset by the news about his mother Lorenzo took both her hands in his. 'I can assure you, my dearest,' he murmured, pulling her gently into his arms 'these things just happen, and she is expected to make a full recovery. She is also looking forward to seeing you, very soon.'

'Oh, no...I'm quite sure she isn't,' Antonia muttered, savouring the strength of his tall, muscular figure. 'I'm sorry if I disrupted your lunch party. I hope everyone wasn't too cross with me?'

He shook his head, his arms tightening about her. 'No— I'm afraid to say that they were mostly furious with *me*!' he explained ruefully. 'Especially when, after hunting high and low through the house for you, following your disappearance, Claudia found that damn newspaper clipping. She's really taken to you,' he added. 'And blames me for mishandling the whole affair. In which she is, of course, quite correct.'

'I really don't know what happened,' Antonia confessed sadly. 'I was just so confused...and, I'm sorry to say, so very jealous of Gina that...'

'There is no reason why you should believe me, of course,' he told her with a heavy sigh. 'But that woman never even came close to denting my heart. Nor, despite what she may have said, did I ever lead her to believe that she had a permanent place in my life—and I certainly never allowed her to move into my apartment.'

'I do believe you,' Antonia muttered. 'It was incredibly stupid of me to listen to her poisonous lies. In fact, I refused to accept most of what she said—until she showed me that newspaper cutting.'

'Now...I don't want to hear any more about Gina—who is now old history,' he said firmly, giving her a quick kiss.

'I am far more concerned about *our* future, Antonia. Flavia warned me that...'

'*Flavia?*'

He nodded. 'I really could not leave Italy until I was sure that my mother would fully recover her health. And I wasn't prepared to phone you, just in case it tipped you over the edge into refusing to ever see me again. So...yes, I have been keeping tabs on you via your sister-in-law. Who has, I may say, been *most* helpful and encouraging,' he added with a laugh as Antonia beat her fists furiously against his hard chest.

'Now, my dearest, you really must watch that temper of yours,' he teased, easily capturing both her hands and lifting them to his lips. 'Now that I am a reformed character...'

'That I don't believe—not for one minute!' she murmured, smiling mistily up into his handsome face, before his dark head came down to possess her lips in a long, lingering kiss of total commitment.

If you enjoyed what you just read,
then we've got an offer you can't resist!

Take 2 bestselling love stories FREE!

Plus get a FREE surprise gift!